Rip had her wrist locked in an iron grip and dragged her so close she could feel the heat of his body.

His eyes flashed hot enough to singe, a muscle in his jaw ticking. Ashley couldn't tell if he wanted to kill her or kiss her, and for a heartbeat she wondered what his mouth would feel like on hers.

"I don't know what you're planning," he said in a harsh whisper as his thumb stroked along the inside of her wrist, "but whatever it is, I'm telling you it's a bad idea. Stand down and walk away from it, Ashley. Do you hear me?"

Her pulse pounded from his touch. From his fury. From the bittersweet sound of her name on his lips. From the jolt of unwelcome desire.

From his blunt order that shook her to the core.

How dare he try to tell her what to do?

Her mission wouldn't end until she stopped Burk's drug-running operation and the man was behind bars or dead.

WYOMING UNDERCOVER ESCAPE

JUNO RUSHDAN

Harlequin

INTRIGUE

For all who served in the Marine Corps. Once a marine,
always a marine. Thank you for your service.

ISBN-13: 978-1-335-45704-2

Wyoming Undercover Escape

Copyright © 2024 by Juno Rushdan

 Harlequin Enterprises ULC
22 Adelaide St. West, 41st Floor
Toronto, Ontario M5H 4E3, Canada
www.Harlequin.com

Printed in Lithuania

Recycling programs
for this product may
not exist in your area.

MIX
Paper | Supporting
responsible forestry
FSC® C021394

Juno Rushdan is a veteran US Air Force intelligence officer and award-winning author. Her books are action-packed and fast-paced. Critics from *Kirkus Reviews* and *Library Journal* have called her work "heart-pounding James Bond-ian adventure" that "will captivate lovers of romantic thrillers." For a free book, visit her website: www.junorushdan.com.

Books by Juno Rushdan

Harlequin Intrigue

Cowboy State Lawmen: Duty and Honor

Wyoming Mountain Investigation
Wyoming Ranch Justice
Wyoming Undercover Escape

Cowboy State Lawmen

Wyoming Winter Rescue
Wyoming Christmas Stalker
Wyoming Mountain Hostage
Wyoming Mountain Murder
Wyoming Cowboy Undercover
Wyoming Mountain Cold Case

Fugitive Heroes: Topaz Unit

Rogue Christmas Operation
Alaskan Christmas Escape
Disavowed in Wyoming
An Operative's Last Stand

Visit the Author Profile page at Harlequin.com.

CAST OF CHARACTERS

Rip Lockwood—Tough as nails, this former marine and current president of the Iron Warriors motorcycle club will stop at nothing to keep a vow he made years ago—protect Ashley Russo and get justice for the murders of both their brothers.

Ashley Russo—This dedicated sheriff's deputy must decide how far she's willing to go for justice. Even if it means teaming up with the biker she's not quite sure she can trust.

Todd Burk—Nicknamed Teflon because the authorities can never get any charges to stick to him. As the leader of the new outlaw motorcycle gang, the Hellhounds, he has declared war on the Iron Warriors and Rip. He will mercilessly eliminate any threats to his drug operation.

Daniel Clark—The sheriff is a reasonable man, but he won't tolerate anyone messing with his deputies.

Mitch Cody—A deputy and good friend of Ashley's.

Holden Powell—Chief deputy of the sheriff's department and best friend of Angelo Russo, who was murdered.

Stryker—President of the Sons of Chaos outlaw motorcycle gang.

Chapter One

Rip Lockwood crossed the field of his elderly landlady's property, heading to his Airstream parked a few hundred feet away, to grab a screwdriver to repair her dishwasher. Wishing he'd worn his jacket in the chilly November night air, he noticed his front door ajar. Only cracked a couple of inches, but he hadn't left it open.

He drew his gun from its holster on his ankle and trained it on the door. Glancing around, he searched for anyone lurking outside as a lookout or any sign of a parked getaway vehicle. Nothing that didn't belong and no one around, from what he could tell.

A slam from inside the trailer, followed by dishes clattering.

Creeping closer, he caught the creaking tread of heavy footfalls across his floor. More than one person. He listened carefully. Two were skulking inside.

"Hurry up," one said from deeper within, trying to keep his voice low.

Rip eased onto the wood deck under the awning and up to the door. Pleased with himself for oiling the hinges last week, he swung the door open wide and rushed inside the Airstream.

Two men—one with a tall, burly frame and the other with an average build—wearing black hoodies and ski masks spun in his direction. The tall one grabbed the microwave from the counter and hurled it at Rip.

He blocked the blow of the sturdy appliance, but a third guy emerged from the bedroom behind him and charged. No way to sidestep the inbound assault in the tight confines, Rip took aim. But the heavyset guy tackled him around the waist. Rip's weapon discharged at the same time, three bullets hitting the ceiling. He and the guy fell out of the trailer, tumbling off the deck while wrestling, and hitting solid, cold ground.

Unfortunately, the stocky guy landed on top of Rip. Another squeeze of the trigger and a shot fired off low to the side, the slug spitting bark from a tree. The thickset man landed a blow across Rip's face before knocking the gun from his hand and sending it sailing across the grass.

Rip threw a hammer fist up into the man's chest, the meaty part of the swinging blow hitting the solar plexus. Gasping for air, the wind knocked from his lungs, the heavy guy fell backward.

The tall one rushed forward with the microwave hoisted overhead, ready to bring it down on Rip's skull. Rip rolled out of the way an instant before the appliance smashed onto the ground. Still on his back, Rip used the position to his advantage and kicked at the other man's knees. Felt a kneecap give way with the snap of broken ligaments. The man hollered in pain.

As Rip tried to climb to his feet, a punch caught him in the ribs. A second fist struck him in the kidney. The thickset guy hit hard, like a boxer. Rip could guess who it was, but rather than focus on identifying him, he needed to immobilize him first. He spun, vision blurring, swinging his elbow up and around, using the added momentum to drive the blow hard into the side of the guy's head. If he'd punched him with that much force, Rip would have broken his hand, whereas his elbow barely registered it.

The heavy guy staggered, clearly disorientated, but he was strong and could take a solid punch. Rip charged straight at him, a wounded bull, lifting the heavy man off his feet and slamming him backward against the ground.

Steel glinted in the moonlight. His gun.

They both went for the weapon.

Then Rip reconsidered. Instead, he launched a fist into his assailant's face, throttling him with jabs until his attacker was dazed.

Where was the third guy?

Adrenaline hot in his veins, Rip reached for his gun. In his peripheral vision he spotted a shadow moving. His fingertips grazed cold steel. The third assailant tried punting his head off with a front kick. Abandoning the gun, Rip jerked away from the incoming boot, but not fast enough. The tip caught him in the jaw.

The tang of blood filled his mouth. He scrambled up onto his hands and knees, reaching for the sheathed Marine Corps KA-BAR on his hip. Or rather, the one that should've been on his belt.

Swearing, he realized he'd left the knife in his trailer.

Mr. Average, who'd gotten in him the jaw, stood with gloved hands clenched and a knapsack on his back. The tall man, now limping, pulled a 9mm gun from his waistband that had been concealed by his sweatshirt.

Rip groped around for something, anything he could use as a weapon, and his fingers closed around a large rock.

"No!" the average one said to the tall guy, his tone sharp with alarm, his palm raised. "Remember, you can't shoot him."

The voice familiar, Rip thought he might be able to pin-point it.

The man holding the gun hesitated. "No, I just can't kill him."

Rip threw the rock, hitting the guy holding the gun square in the forehead. The man swore, stumbling backward and holding his head with one hand while maintaining a shaky grip on the pistol with the other. Rip spun on to his knees, ready to lunge.

A shotgun cocked, not too far in the distance, pumping a shell into the chamber. The sound was loud and unmistakable. "You're trespassing!" Mrs. Ida Hindley called out. She was his landlady and friend and the closest thing to family that Rip had left. "You better leave because I shoot to kill."

That warning was meant for Rip. He dropped to the ground before Ida opened fire. She could only see a few feet clearly in front of her and that was in bright light. Eighty big steps away, at night, she was just as likely to shoot him as his attackers.

The shotgun cracked, sounding like a mini explosion, the shell getting dangerously close to the big guy.

The three assailants took off toward the woods, one hobbling impressively fast.

Ida pumped off one deafening shot after another, changing her aim each time, determined to hit something. Even if it only ended up being trees and his trailer.

The men disappeared into the darkness.

Motorcycle engines grumbled to life, the sound faint, the sight of the bikes concealed by the woods. They must've been parked on the auxiliary road near the property. Seconds later, the bikes sped off, and Ida was finally out of ammo.

Rip lumbered to his feet and started making his way to Ida. She had lowered the shotgun to her side, but better to be safe than sorry. "It's only me," he said, in case she had extra shells in the pockets of her robe. "They're gone."

Getting closer, he spotted her late husband's snub-nosed revolver in her other hand.

"Are you all right?" she asked.

"I'll live." He slipped the shotgun from her trembling hand, touched his jaw and winced. "You're going to kill someone one day."

"Only a trespasser who deserves it." Giving him a sly grin, she took the arm he offered, and they headed to her house. "I dare anyone to doubt that I would, son." Even with her frail body racked with rheumatoid arthritis, white hair in rollers, wearing winter boots and a flannel bathrobe over pajamas, she was a formidable woman who shouldn't be tested.

"Well, I'm not fool enough to doubt you, Auntie Ida." They might not be related by blood but were still kin.

Shoving the revolver in her pocket, she wheezed, and he slowed their pace.

Tragedy had claimed the lives of their closest relatives. When he was a young teen, Ida had taken him in along with his younger brother. Despite her love and lectures and desperation to keep them away from the motorcycle club their father had been a part of, they had joined the Iron Warriors MC anyway.

If only they had listened.

If only they hadn't chased after some illusory birthright.

If only Rip hadn't failed to protect his brother, he might still be alive.

If only...

"Now, what was all the ruckus about?" she asked.

"MC business," he said.

"Iron Warriors business or Hellhounds?"

The Iron Warriors were his, at least those who still wore the MC cut displaying their patches and insignia, and he had their unwavering loyalty. The Hellhounds, the newly formed OMG, outlaw motorcycle gang, were his cross to bear.

Somehow Todd Burk had dragged the club so deep into illicit and illegal activity, right under his nose, that Rip had to put a stop to it, drawing a line in the sand. In the end, Rip had made a mess of things and caused his club to split.

Those who agreed that they should not deal drugs stood with him as Iron Warriors. The vast majority who didn't, who loved the money, who craved power and refused to give any of it up, had broken away with Burk as their leader and become the Hellhounds.

The group's existence was yet another failure Rip had to atone for and deal with.

He helped Ida up the steps of her back porch and inside the house. "It's best if that's all you know." Gently, he set her down in a chair.

"There's been a lot of ugly, unfortunate *MC business* around here and in town lately." Ida was back up on her feet, plodding to the refrigerator. She grabbed milk and went to the stove.

"Precisely why I don't want you to pull another stunt like that," he said, setting the shotgun on the kitchen counter. "Understand? I don't want you to get hurt."

She waved a dismissive hand at him. "I've had eighty-nine good years on this earth. They weren't always easy, but I've gotten to see the world, make my mark on it, known the love of family and cherished friends." She put a delicate hand on his arm and squeezed. "What I will not do is hide in here while someone I care about is in danger out there." She pointed through the window at the land in the direction of his trailer.

"I don't want you to risk your life for mine." No one should die to save him.

Giving a dry chuckle, she poured milk in a pan and turned on the fire. "Remind me, how old are you?" She counted on her fingers. "Thirty-five?"

"You flatter me. Thirty-eight."

She opened a cabinet and grabbed hot chocolate. "My life has been full and rich, though not with money." Another dry laugh. "When my time comes, I'll be ready. And I want you to be at peace with it. But you've got more than half your life ahead of you, son."

Things had only escalated with Burk, going from bad to worse. Rip had been extorted, shot at, and had his tires slashed. No matter how hard he tried to avoid bloodshed that would only lead to a war, he wasn't so sure he'd outlive Ida. And after tonight's incident, with her getting involved, he'd reached a crossroads.

If he allowed this mayhem to continue, Ida would be burying him before the new year.

"I wouldn't be so sure about that." He dug out the cold compress from the freezer and put it on his face. "I haven't done much good with the first half of my life." Maybe there wasn't much point in the second half. "What do I have to show for it?"

"You left this small town and the club to join the military because I begged you to."

And he'd also left his brother behind, who refused to leave.

Rip had seen the dark side of the MC culture and when Auntie Ida pleaded, no, *dared* him to see what else there might be in the world for him, he didn't back down from the challenge.

Ida got out mini marshmallows and caramel syrup and

set them on the counter, but not the chocolate syrup when she knew he liked a drizzle of both on his cocoa.

He was lucky to have her in his life, someone willing to shoot his attackers and make him hot chocolate. Dropping into a chair, he propped an elbow on his leg, resting his head in his hand, and put the compress to his face.

"You saved lives in the Marines," Ida continued. "Looking around here, you can't see it. But dig out your Navy Cross and look at that. It's proof you made an impact. Not only on those you saved, but for their mothers and fathers and siblings and spouses and children. You also came back home to make an even bigger difference." He opened his mouth to protest, and she raised her palm, silencing him. "You haven't achieved what you set out to do. Not yet." She handed him a cup of hot cocoa. "Not yet," she repeated. "But there's still time. And where there's a will, there's a way. Even if we don't like the way forward or it happens to be unexpected, there comes a point where we have to make a choice. Do we keep at it, using the same methods that haven't worked. Or find a new way to fight."

There was time. As a Marine Raider, he was trained to deal with disaster and eliminate too many types of enemies to name. Stopping terrorists was his specialty. He was going to use his skill set and whatever time he had left to take down Todd Burk.

War wasn't a possibility that he could prevent. It was already on his doorstep, and he was in the thick of it. But the one thing he knew how to do was fight a war.

He needed to be ruthless to win. Even if doing so killed him.

Ida picked up two mugs and left the kitchen.

"Why did you make three cups of cocoa?" How did he not notice until now?

She shuffled down the hallway and he followed behind her.

Red-and-blue flashing lights pulled up in front of the house.

"You called the sheriff's department?" he asked. Irritation sparked through him. "I can't talk to the law about MC business."

No one snitched. Not even about this. That was the code. They lived by it. Died by it. Honored it. Even a legit biker and upstanding citizen like him did not get the authorities involved.

"But I got the pretty deputy to come," she said.

Gritting his teeth, Rip sighed. There were a couple of female deputies in the sheriff's department, but instantly he knew she was talking about the gorgeous one he had a complicated relationship with. "You asked for the one who hates me?"

And Ashley Russo had every reason to despise him, the club and everything the MC stood for. No matter how hard he'd tried to break down her wall of disdain—and he'd tried very, very hard—it was never enough to get her to change the way she looked at him.

There was a rap at the door. Light from the headlights and flashing strobes outlined a slender athletic shape wearing a cowboy hat through the glass pane of the door.

"I thought you two had some kind of thing going on. That you were at least friends," Ida said.

"Friends trust each other. That's not the case here. We've formed a tenuous…" He was at a loss for what to call it. Association? Acquaintance? Civility? No word was quite right. "I guess we do have some kind of a *thing*." But it was held together by gossamer threads. One wrong move on his part and it would snap.

"That does explain all the questions she asked me a few weeks ago about whether you were living on the property against my will and if you were paying a reasonable rent or if I wanted you to leave. But I cleared it up. Set her straight about you. She gave me her card, with her personal cell phone number on the back, and told me to call her anytime, especially if there was trouble. So I did, tonight."

"What? Why didn't you tell me? When was she here?" *How was any of that friendly?*

Another knock. This time louder.

Ida looked at him with a wry grin. "There's a thin line between love and hate. Now open the door and act like the man I raised you to be."

"She blames me for the death of her brother," he admitted, his voice low.

He remembered like it was yesterday, the conversation Ashley had overheard at her brother's funeral, the way she came up to him, a fearless seventeen-year-old girl, slapped his face, pounded on his chest and screamed her anger and grief.

Ida's smile fell. "Is she justified?"

Rip didn't pull the trigger but shared the blame for Angelo's death and for his own brother's. "In a way, yes."

"Then it's high time you took responsibility for it and started righting your wrongs."

Scratching his head, he wished Ida had warned him she had called the authorities. More specifically, one deputy in particular.

Ida switched on the porch light and the one in the foyer and gave him a *get-on-with-it* look.

Dropping the cold compress onto a side table, Rip stalked up to the door and opened it. His gaze met the deputy's, her whiskey-brown eyes narrowing a fraction. He gave her the once-over, surprised she wasn't in uniform. Her dark hair hung loose, falling past her shoulders rather than pulled into a ponytail or the tight braid she sported whenever he'd seen her working. Form-fitting jeans accentuated her long legs and rounded hips. A tucked-in flannel shirt and leather jacket didn't do much to flatter her figure. But her classic hourglass shape on her five-foot-seven frame made it impossible to ignore the fact she was no longer a girl.

He flicked a glance over her shoulder. She had driven her personal truck, using portable red-and-blue emergency lights that could easily be mounted to the dash or windshield with suction cups, rather than a patrol SUV. "Are you off duty?"

The deputy unhooked her badge from her belt and held it up, making it clear she was working even if she might be off duty.

"I'll ask the questions." She gestured past him into the house.

The star in her hand reminded him what he *didn't* like about her. Rip stepped aside, opening the door wide.

She came in, bringing with her the cold and the crisp, clean scent of frost.

Ida handed the deputy a mug. "I made it just the way you like it. With mini marshmallows and caramel syrup."

"Thank you," she said. "But you shouldn't have gone to the trouble."

Rip glanced down at his mug. He had neither the zhuzh of marshmallows nor syrup.

Sipping his plain cocoa, he shut the door and followed them down the hall. His gaze slipped below the deputy's waistline and belt with flashlight, pepper spray, handcuffs and holstered gun, and locked onto the gentle sway of her hips. He liked her curves, and she had plenty of them. Appreciated the strength of her body from a combat standpoint. But he had to fight against the primal physical interest, the spark of heat that flashed inside him whenever she was near.

Inside the kitchen, he hurried to the table and helped Ida ease down into a chair. In the evenings her arthritis got worse, making her stiff.

The deputy glanced around the room, her gaze lingering on the shotgun on the counter, and took out a notepad and pen. "I'm responding to a report of shots fired. The best way for me to do my job efficiently is if you're honest when answering my questions," she said, all business, staring right at him as she spoke. "You might not be a Marine anymore, but tonight I need you to abide by the same uncompromising integrity of the corps instead of your MC code of silence."

"Once a Marine, always a Marine," he said, not turning away from her face, which he liked even more than her figure.

Satin-smooth complexion. The golden brown hue of her skin showed her multiracial heritage. Italian on her father's side. Creole on her mother's. Not that it was one thing about her, like her high cheekbones, but rather the complete package, the sum of her parts, that he found captivating. He could look at her for hours and often struggled not to stare.

"A distinguished Marine," Ida chimed in, her voice full of pride. "Ripton lives by a set of core values that have formed the bedrock of his character."

"Really? Is that so?" The deputy didn't filter the sharp skepticism from her tone. "What kind of core values?"

He understood the law enforcement game she was playing. When a cop thought they might have trouble getting answers from a person, they warmed them up, getting them talking about something the reluctant party was comfortable with first.

Unfortunately for her, he'd been playing this game far longer and was better at it.

"I do my best never to lie unless there's good cause. But I never cheat. Never steal. Don't break the law." Honor, strength to do what was right, commitment—an unrelenting determination to achieve victory in every endeavor—made him who he was.

He'd tried to tell her this before but she either didn't listen or didn't believe him.

"I only hope that's true." She stepped closer, dangerously close, inches separating them, studying his face as if searching for the truth, and heat flared again, coaxing him to thaw. Enticing him to strive for something far deeper than friendship with her.

But he backed away from the deputy, going around to the other side of the table. Regardless of how attractive he found her or how drawn to her he was, or that he needed to, and intended to, make amends for her brother, he had to be the same with her right now as he would be with any other badge investigating. Stone-cold.

An iceberg that wouldn't crack.

Chapter Two

Staring up at Ripton Lockwood, with her being at least six inches shorter than him, Ashley fully expected him to answer every question with a half-truth or simply evade giving a real answer at all. He might still consider himself a Marine, but instead of wearing a military uniform, he usually wore a biker cut.

Though he didn't have on the leather vest covered in patches now.

He was not only a member of a notorious motorcycle club but also the president of the Iron Warriors.

The MC had been a blight in the towns of Laramie and Bison Ridge for as long as she could remember. Corrupting the youth, recruiting them into their ranks with sparkly promises, neglecting to disclose that not everything that glitters was gold.

A few things gave her a glimmer of hope that Rip might be honest about tonight's events and, if so, possibly help her with her one-woman crusade. Ida Hindley's high praise of him. The DEA's recent deep-dive background report on him that only showed two red flags: his motorcycle club affiliation and no verifiable source of legitimate income. There was also the fact most of his rotten-apple bikers had broken away, forming a new, dangerous faction—the

Hellhounds—under Todd Burk. The man who had brutally killed her brother.

Now the Hellhounds seemed hell-bent on putting Rip six feet under.

Maybe the enemy of her enemy could be a real ally?

The way he answered her questions would tell her. "Mrs. Hindley told me you were fixing her dishwater, left to get a tool from your trailer, and then she heard gunshots."

Rip stared down at her with that uneasy stillness to him. He possessed a coiled readiness, a wariness that made her nerves hum, giving him a more lethal vibe than any other MC gang member. Nothing on the job ever made her nervous.

But he did.

He wasn't quite like the other bikers. Guarded, sure, but he didn't taunt authority as though invincible, certainly didn't back down from it, and he didn't run in a pack.

For all the years she'd seen him around, she'd usually encountered him alone. More baffling was his living situation with Mrs. Hindley. Apparently, Rip had taken care of her debts, saving the land she was about to lose due to outstanding unpaid property taxes, and still paid her rent.

The question was where did he get the money?

He didn't have a nine-to-five job, and whenever she asked about employment, he'd given cagey responses.

The elderly woman had been eager to explain why Rip had done so much for her, but Ashley had been called away to respond to a 10-80, chase in progress.

She was bound and determined to figure out what Rip's deal was.

"That's right," Mrs. Hindley said, holding her cocoa between her hands. "And then I called you."

Instead of 911, which puzzled Ashley, but she wasn't going to squander this rare opportunity.

"Walk me through what happened," she said.

Rip pushed up the sleeves of his shirt, revealing corded forearms and tattoos, then pulled out a chair for her to sit. His gaze never left her, always watchful. Especially of her.

She decided to change course. "Why don't you show me where the altercation happened while you walk me through it?"

"Out at my Airstream." He turned to Ida. "Will you be all right until I get back?"

Sipping her cocoa, Ida waved a hand at him. "I don't need a babysitter. You're the one who needs looking after."

Grabbing his black sheepskin bomber jacket from a hook, Rip smiled and gave a low, husky chuckle far sexier than Ashley wanted it to be. He opened the back door and, standing against the jamb on the threshold, held it for her.

She hesitated.

Not that she feared him. Oddly, not once had he ever made her afraid. She simply didn't care for his politeness, how careful he was never to stand too close—*she was the one always stepping within arm's reach, maybe to test him*—the way he seemed aware of his height and strength and how intimidating it could be.

The dark jeans and gray Henley he wore did little to hide his sculpted chest and muscled arms. Another stark reminder of his physical capabilities.

If only he acted less chivalrous and more despicable, it would be easier to cling to her lingering doubts about him.

"You'll be safe in the dark alone with me, Deputy. Don't worry, I won't bite. Unless you want me to." His slow grin made her skin tingle.

It was devilish and inviting, and she had to fight very hard not to grin back at his effortless charm.

She'd been alone with him plenty of times and always

felt safe, but they'd never been together in the dark. This flirty banter of his was just a game, so she decided to play by putting her hand on the hilt of her gun. "I'm not worried because I'm armed."

Ashley brushed past him, their bodies grazing, and she couldn't ignore the hard, rugged wall of muscle beneath his clothes. The smell of him. Soap and leather and pine. Up close, his eyes were a startling blue-gray that commanded attention. His features were sharp and chiseled, his square jaw unshaven. The sheer size of him never had her strategizing how best to take him down if necessary, because she didn't consider him a personal threat.

In fact, whenever she drew near him, her stomach fluttered as it did now.

Instantly, she became aware of her mistake. Physical contact. She wished she'd had him lead the way and gone out behind him.

Rip might be ridiculously—*disarmingly*—good-looking, but she refused to be attracted to a selfish man who ran from responsibility when he could have prevented her brother's death.

He shut the back door and slipped on his jacket.

Ashley walked beside him. "How long have you lived here?"

"Depends on the perspective."

An answer that told her nothing. He was good at giving those. "I need to know for my investigation and the report. You agreed to cooperate."

"Did I?" He raised an eyebrow. "Don't think so."

She thought back to the brief conversation in the kitchen. He was right. "You said you wouldn't lie."

"I said I do my best not to." He flipped up the collar of his jacket against the wind. "And I haven't lied to you. *Ever.*"

Another flutter whipped through her on his last word, but she deliberately tamped it down. "Why did you call me if you're only going to stonewall?"

"Ida called you. Not me."

She stopped walking. Once he did too, she hiked her chin up at him. "Would you prefer a different deputy to handle this?"

Shoving his hands in his pockets, with a hint of a smile on his face, he stared at her. That incisive, intense gaze and the sharp intelligence behind it made her squirm a little on the inside.

"I'd prefer none at all," he said, running his fingers across his head. Gone was his slightly too long sable hair that fell past his collar in favor of a buzz cut that made him look harder, edgier. Sexier.

"I already called it in to the station. So, it's me or someone else."

"You're in civilian clothes and driving your personal vehicle. Why are you here off duty?"

Technically, she wasn't off duty. For the past couple of months, she'd worked around the clock on a special assignment. "Ida called. I told her that if she ever needed me, I would come."

"Because you're worried about me?"

Odd way to phrase it. "Because I'm worried about her with you."

His jaw twitched as he seemed to chew on that. "I prefer you. Over the others. Since I've got no choice." He turned and continued to his trailer.

At the Airstream, she pulled latex gloves from her pocket, slipped them on and looked around outside, noting the damaged microwave oven on the ground.

Rip picked up a gun and held it up by the hilt. "It's mine.

Discharged four times. Once out here, hitting a tree. The other three inside the trailer into the ceiling."

She opened an evidence bag, and he dropped the sub-compact gun—SIG P365, she guessed—inside. "I thought you'd be a good shot, as a Marine."

"I am. When I intend to shoot, I don't miss. All the shots were accidental. The discharge happened during a scuffle."

She glanced at his hips. No holster. "Where were you carrying?" she asked, shaking the bag.

Pulling up his pant leg, he revealed an ankle holster.

"Got a concealed carry permit?"

He took his wallet from his inner jacket pocket and fished it out.

She looked it over. The permit was in order. She handed it back to him. "Shouldn't have your gun too long. This is only a formality. Procedure. I'll call you when you can get it back." His number was one of the few she had programmed in her phone, though she rarely had reason to use it. "Why do you live way out here, so far from town, on Mrs. Hindley's land?" she asked, trying again now that he was talking.

Since age nineteen, Ashley had lived in Bison Ridge, away from town, in the house her grandmother had bequeathed her. It was peaceful, surrounded by nature. Not unlike here.

"It's an arrangement that works for both of us."

Still being cagey.

"I noticed your motorcycle parked at Mrs. Hindley's house instead of in your driveway out here." The suspects would have heard his engine approaching and probably would've hightailed it out of there before he got close enough for an altercation if they only wanted to rob him or trash his place. "Why?"

"Ida needed a refill on her blood pressure medication. She wanted me to wait until the morning to get it, but I insisted since the pharmacy in town was still open. I parked at the house when I got back. We chatted for a while. Then she wanted me to look at the dishwasher because it had started leaking."

"Walk me through what happened," she said, and Rip explained everything from finding his door open to Mrs. Hindley firing her shotgun. "Can you describe what they looked like?"

"They wore ski masks, black hoodies and gloves. One was average height and build. The other was an inch taller than me but with slightly less bulk. The third one was thick around the middle. Stocky."

"Any distinguishing marks? Visible tattoos?"

"No. But the tall one is limping after the altercation."

"Did you recognize their voices?"

He hesitated and then shook his head. "Can't put a definitive name to any of them."

His choice of words had been careful. Too careful. "But you have some idea who they might be?"

"I don't care to speculate. Sorry, Deputy."

But if he did, no doubt he'd name three Hellhounds.

Sighing, she stepped inside the trailer and looked around. It was in a shambles. Broken dishes on the floor. Cushions ripped open and stuffing pulled out. The mess would take a solid day to clean up and furniture would have to be replaced.

Three guys to trash one trailer was a lot. Overkill really, unless they'd wanted the backup in case they encountered Rip. Three against one and he'd done substantial damage. Impressive.

"Did they take anything?" she asked.

He stood near the door under the bullet holes. "I haven't had a chance to look, but I don't have anything of value. I don't keep cash in here."

She walked over to him. "What about drugs?"

"I don't do drugs. Never used. Never dealt it. Also, don't condone the trafficking of it."

She searched his face and, strangely, believed him. If he was into drugs, she supposed he'd give her one of his *non-answer answers* to avoid lying.

Passing him on her way back outside, she caught the masculine smell of him again. Her body tightened against it. Outside, she was grateful for the fresh air.

"You know this is a crime." She gestured at the trailer.

"What, assault with a microwave?" he asked, the corner of his mouth hitching up.

She bit back a smile. "I wasn't referring to that." She pointed higher, to the colorful pepper-shaped lights strung up along the awning on the outside of the Airstream. This was her first time at his home, and she realized how little she knew about him. "Putting up Christmas decorations before Thanksgiving."

The holiday feast at her parents' house would be next week. This was the hardest time of year for her, for the entire family, since her brother had been killed right after Halloween.

"You're one of those, huh? A believer that the holidays shall not overlap. Ida is the same. She calls the lights sacrilege. But I like having them up for longer than a month. The festive feel of it, though I've got nothing to celebrate."

She eyed him for a moment. "We can sweep for fingerprints, but since they wore gloves, I doubt we'll get any other than yours and those of visitors."

"No visitors. Not even Ida comes in here."

"No lady friends?"

He leaned against the side of the trailer, that laser focus of his full bore on her. "Are you asking as part of your investigation?"

Honestly, she wasn't sure why she'd asked. "Curious."

"No lady friends, Deputy."

"You mean that you bring here. I guess that's what your clubhouse is for." The MC had a clubhouse, if it should be called such, that Rip had built. Once again, raising the question of how it was paid for if not by illicit means? A massive single-story building that took up almost half a block. She'd heard the rumor that every member had his own bedroom at the club. After they partied hard, everyone had a private space to sleep or continue having fun with a woman. Not only that, but they also reportedly had a bar, game room, armory, conference room, gym, and a stage with stripper poles. *Classy.*

"If that's what you want to think, go ahead, but you'd be wrong about me."

"Why so cryptic?" She wasn't inquiring about MC secrets, only if there was a woman in his life, or occasionally in his bed. Not that she cared either way.

"Why so curious?" he countered.

"Can't help it." Particularly when it came to him. "It's what I do—ask questions, investigate, solve problems."

"I meant no lady friends. Period. Before you ask, no, I'm not gay. Only single. And when the clubhouse belonged to the Iron Warriors, I never used the room designated for me to sleep with women."

Something important in his comment registered.

"What do you mean *when* the clubhouse belonged to the Iron Warriors?" The answer dawned on her, but it didn't make any sense. "The clubhouse belongs to the Hell-hounds now?"

A shadow crossed his eyes. "I gave it to them."

"What?" That wasn't akin to giving a bully your lunch or the money in your wallet, but more extreme, like giving them your entire house or life savings. "Why?"

Rip wasn't the type to roll over and give in. Was he?

Her gut clenched at what this could mean. The Iron Warriors were losing the battle against the Hellhounds. Rip was losing.

Where would that leave the town? If Rip and his guys were a blight, then Burk and his posse were a plague.

"The answer to that question is none of your concern," he said, his tone matter-of-fact, his stance unyielding. "Has no relevance on your investigation."

"It's connected. Todd forming a new gang. You giving him your clubhouse. The clubhouse you built for them. The other day, Ida told me someone slashed your tires. And now this. I'm sure there's now one Hellhound with a limp. Be honest with me."

"You want the truth?"

"Yes."

"Move on," he said, and she caught the warning as well as the worry in his voice. "Ida only called you tonight because she thought I might be in trouble or hurt. I'm fine."

She squared her shoulders, irritated at his straightforward manner of telling her zilch. Glancing back at the trailer, she tried to regroup. "Deputy Livingston will be out to sweep for prints. Maybe one of them got sloppy and we'll get lucky."

"Not necessary. I'd prefer not to have any further intrusion in my home if we can avoid it."

Frustration welled inside her. "Can I give you some advice?"

"Certainly. Doesn't mean I'll take it."

"In this turf battle between the Iron Warriors and Hell-hounds, don't become a person of interest." She needed him free to help her, not investigated or locked up behind bars.

"Well, I *am* an interesting person."

She sighed, her breath crystallizing in the air. "Anything else you can tell me about what happened here tonight?"

"Nothing. And believe me, I wish I could."

"Thanks for the paperwork I'll have to do tonight since I have to file a report that will lead to nothing." She put away her notepad. "If you find anything missing, let me know."

Little point to her coming out here, let alone looking at his trailer, though it was nice to finally see where he lived. Maybe she could make this trip worth her while. She had to ask him sooner or later for help and couldn't wait for him to make another random visit to her house.

"Sorry about the paperwork and that I couldn't be more helpful," he said, almost sounding sincere. "I wish I hadn't taken up so much of your time while you're off duty, Deputy."

His politeness and formality were galling.

"You and I have history," she said. He owed her for her brother's death, and she was going to make him clear that debt. But over the years, he'd watched out for her and cease-lessly endeavored to build something beyond their complicated bond of obligation. In the back of her mind, she couldn't be sure he wasn't trying to use her. A powerful thing if a motorcycle club president had a cop in his pocket.

"That we do," he agreed.

"You show up at my house maybe twice a month to check in on me." Sometimes it was closer to every eight to ten days. Rip seemed to always be doing that. Looking out for her. Making sure she was okay. At first, they only talked outside on her porch. Then he started bringing food—tacos, empanadas, savory croissants from the café, delectable, irresistible items that got him inside the house, and once even a bottle of whiskey. She'd told him she preferred tequila. For her recent—twenty-fifth—birthday, instead of giving her the usual bath oils, luxury candles or silk kimono robes that she loved but would never buy for herself, he'd given her a bottle of Clase Azul twenty-fifth anniversary tequila. Someone at the office told her it cost three thousand dollars. Good thing she hadn't mentioned who'd given it to her, or they would've thought it was a bribe. That was what she'd suspected after learning the price. "It's weird, the way you only call me Deputy. Even when we bump into each other in town and I'm in plainclothes. Or when you're at my house."

He always parked around back, like his presence at her home was a dirty secret, and maybe for her it was, but she never let him past her kitchen.

She'd been grateful for the distance the use of her title provided, preventing them from ever getting too close, but now she needed that distance erased.

Rip folded his arms. "That's what you are."

"It's my job title. Not *who* I am." In a small town, it was hard to be someone else once you clocked out of your job, but she didn't always have to be Deputy Russo. "Use my first name. When you do, I'll know you haven't forgotten. About my brother. About the misery you could've prevented."

Something flashed across his face. Guilt? Pain? Whatever it was, it was real, honest.

"I haven't forgotten," he said. "I'll never forget. Burk will pay for Angelo. For everything. I swear it."

The words hit her, not as a blow, but more as a sudden, swift bear hug. Strong and reassuring.

He was a hardened Marine who had sworn to defend his country—once he'd even sworn to protect her, too, on the day her brother was buried. Back then, she couldn't hear it, wouldn't believe it. Now she suspected Rip didn't take oaths lightly.

Still, she didn't trust him completely either, which put her in a difficult position, because she was going to have to put her life in his hands.

"Why do you live here? Mrs. Hindley is itching to tell me." Ashley needed Rip to share, to open up further. DEA Agent Welliver had hammered home the importance of it when trying to cultivate an asset. Oddly, it made her wonder if that was what Rip had been up to all this time, with the visits to her house, asking her personal questions—trying to recruit her, but to what end? "I want to hear it from you. Will you give me that?"

He sighed. "My parents died when I was thirteen. Ida took us in, me and my brother, Thatcher. *Hatch*, that's what everyone called him. She cared for us when no one else would. She had lost her husband and her daughter and needed someone to love. Would've been less heartache for her if she'd rescued a couple of stray dogs instead and let us go to foster care." The regret in his voice was thick.

His candor touched something deep inside of her she hadn't expected.

"I'm out here to look after her," he continued. "To give her what company I can. Fix whatever breaks. Get her groceries. Make sure she takes her medication. She needs me now, though she'd spin a different tale, so I'm here."

Rip was an enigma. He'd told her things about himself, details that painted him as a good guy. A great one in fact.

All of which she doubted and questioned until talking to Ida. Ashley had seen many things that made her wonder why he was ever in the MC, much less a club president. Sponsoring blood drives, holding fundraisers for the elementary school to cover the cost of pre-kindergarten, the way he was helping Ida when he didn't have to. How he watched out for Ashley. Not once had she had any problems with the Iron Warriors since he took over the club. Rip was both laudable and lamentable.

She struggled to reconcile the dichotomy.

"What happened to your brother?" She knew that Hatch had tried to rob a strip club one night while drunk, with some other bikers. He'd been caught and, while in prison, someone had killed him. Stabbed him with a shiv. According to the report, one of the guards suspected it had been related to a drug deal.

If Burk had been involved, Rip might let something slip.

His lips firmed. "I failed him. The same way I failed yours."

Ashley approached him, cautiously, as one would a wild animal being cornered. Not that she expected him to attack her. But her situation meant risking her life all the same. She couldn't afford to make a mistake. Not with him.

She drew as close as possible without touching him and could see the stormy blue-gray of his eyes in the illumination from the string lights above his head.

He stiffened, pressing his back to the side of the trailer as though he wanted to get away from her. But he didn't walk off, only shoved his hands in his pockets.

"I need your help," she said, her voice a hair above a whisper, even though they were alone.

His brows pinched together. "With what?" His tone matched hers.

"Taking down Burk, once and for all."

Straightening to his full height, he leaned in a little. "I warned you to stay away from him. Told you I'd handle it."

"Yeah, seven years ago. How has that been going for nearly a decade?" she asked, and he lowered his gaze. "You don't get to do that. I want you to look at me."

He lifted his head, his eyes meeting hers, but everything about him frosted over, putting distance between them, even though they were only inches apart. Might as well have been miles.

"I'm going after him," she continued. "But I need you." She had to be careful about how much to tell him until he agreed to help her.

"*Need*, huh. Tempting words coming from you," he said with sudden, cool remoteness that still managed to warm her. "But I'm not sure what you're saying. Are you asking to get dirty with me?"

Ashley hated the power he had over her, to make her belly flutter or her thighs tingle with the slightest innuendo. She cursed him in her head. "I have sensitive information I'm going to act on. I could use your help."

"I can't work with a cop. Cooperation is one thing. Collaboration is quite another. The code—"

"Forget about the MC code. For once. Please."

He stared at her for a long moment, as if looking straight through her, down to her soul.

When he didn't respond, she asked, "Did you mean it when you said you'd protect me?"

He gave a curt nod. "Of course."

"Then help me," she implored with every fiber of her being. It might be the only way she could take down Burk's operation and get out alive. "Do you have any idea what this takes?" To her chagrin, she heard her voice threaten to break and he dropped his head back against the trailer. "For me to come to you and ask? Please, I need you on this."

"I can't." His jaw tightened. "Just leave this to me. I'll handle it," Rip said, anger or annoyance edging his voice.

"When? In the next seven years? Seven days? Do you even have a week? Because you can't handle anything if you're dead. Tonight was only a taste of what's to come. Burk is turning up the heat on you. The word around town is it won't stop until you're finished. As in cold in the ground." She studied him, hoping to see a crack in the ice wall he'd thrown up between them. Nothing. "Forget it. I knew asking you was a waste of time. I'll do it on my own."

She spun on her heel, but before she could take two steps, he caught her wrist and whirled her back around, stealing her breath.

It was the first time he'd ever laid a finger on her. At her brother's funeral, she'd wailed as she thrashed him, beating him with her fists, and he'd done nothing to stop her or defend himself. He'd simply taken it until her parents had hauled her off him.

But now he had her wrist locked in an iron grip and dragged her so close she could feel the heat of his body. His eyes flashed hot enough to singe, a muscle in his jaw ticking. His face was so near hers his chocolaty breath brushed across her lips. She couldn't tell if he wanted to kill her or kiss her, and for a heartbeat she wondered what his mouth would feel like on hers.

"I don't know what you're planning," he said in a harsh whisper as his thumb stroked along the inside of her wrist. "But whatever it is, I'm telling you it's a bad idea. Stand down and walk away from it, Ashley. Do you hear me?"

Her pulse pounded from his touch. From his fury. From

the bittersweet sound of her name on his lips. From the jolt of unwelcome desire.

From his blunt order that shook her to the core.

How dare he try to tell her what to do?

She was no longer a teenage girl. She had been with the sheriff's department since she was of legal age to join. For nearly seven years, she'd worn the badge and done as he asked, staying away from Todd Burk, his MC brother, while he *handled* it. Not anymore. She was done waiting. "Shame on you. For asking me to back down. For not helping me, when I have never asked you for anything. I've finally got a chance to stop Burk and I'm taking it. I'll handle it while you keep running from your responsibility."

Ashley yanked her arm free from his tight grasp and marched off toward her truck.

DEA Agent Welliver had given her the tip she'd been waiting for. The final piece had been Rip, but...

Shaking her head, she whisked away her disappointment. She didn't need him. It would be riskier without him, a lot riskier, but she could do it alone.

Come hell or high water, she wasn't going to be like Rip. She wasn't going to fail.

Her mission wouldn't end until she stopped Burk's drug-running operation and the man was behind bars or dead.

Chapter Three

Pushing through the front door of the first-ever Iron Warriors clubhouse, Rip hated the emotions running riot through him. Anger. Shame. Defeat.

No. Only a temporary setback.

Rip had lost a battle, but not the war.

Taking off his sunglasses, he sat in a rickety chair and looked around. In the early afternoon light, the ultra-rural cabin situated in the middle of nowhere looked even more dilapidated. Almost a twenty-minute drive outside of Laramie or Bison Ridge, it was a sufficient spot for privacy, to gather with his men and strategize without any of their plans getting leaked.

For far too long, Rip had been trying to take care of the problem named Todd Burk, without any of his other brothers in the MC being collateral damage.

The task had proved impossible.

Todd had layers and layers of separation from most of the illegal activity, insulation by the very men Rip had been trying to protect.

The sheriff's department had done half the work of cleaning up the club, without Rip's involvement, by shutting down Burk's prostitution ring with help from the FBI. Todd had a few civilian sleazeballs running the day-to-day of handling the women and clients. Two low-level Iron Warriors had been collecting the money, funneling it back to Todd. They were arrested but refused to incriminate Burk.

Nasty business that had opened Rip's eyes to what had been transpiring unbeknownst to him. A couple of months later, he learned about the drug trafficking when his own brother was killed. Hatch had been behind bars for armed robbery, serving nine years. A dangerous, foolish act that never would've happened if Rip had been around instead of serving in the military. Hatch kept getting into trouble in prison and his sentence extended with every infraction. Then his brother had gotten caught in the middle of a turf war between rival gangs selling narcotics behind bars. That was how Rip discovered Todd had been sneaking drugs into the prison somehow and turned Hatch into a dealer.

Rip had dug around with the type of professional scrutiny he'd used in the Marines.

Todd's operation was extensive. Not only was he dealing locally, but also to every university and college within a four-hour drive of town, poisoning communities and killing kids.

What Rip hadn't been able to ascertain was Todd's supplier, the schedule and location of major shipments, how the cash flowed and was being laundered. He also couldn't prove that Todd was behind any of it. Rip could only decree that the club would not mess with drugs. No transporting or dealing them.

But Todd had been prepared and called the decision to a vote.

One Rip lost.

Those same guys he'd been trying to protect had stabbed him in the back, figuratively, siding with Todd and trading in their Iron Warrior cuts to be Hellhounds.

Now Rip would get as ruthless as required to complete the job, even if it meant half of the new OMG ended up behind bars. A necessary sacrifice as long as he kept Ashley out of the fray.

He looked over at the few men seated that he had left, a whopping four, whom he'd called together this afternoon.

"Meeting here feels like a slap in the face," said Quill, his vice president. A senior Warrior twenty years older than Rip, Quill had seen the club go through many phases and lots of change, but even he was having difficulty with this one. "Being in this run-down shack while the *Hellhounds*—" he spit on the floor "—are in the house that you built."

To clean up the club and steer it toward the straight and narrow path, Rip had to give them a way to earn money. Legitimately. He fell back on what he knew. Combat and defense. He'd formed the Ironside Protection Service. Whether someone needed a single bodyguard or full squad detail, conspicuous or covert, Ironside answered the call. Once they developed a solid reputation, work had begun to pour in, the gigs had gotten better, more lucrative. They had raked in plenty, to pay for the tricked-out clubhouse, to keep them flush in cash and, he had thought, mistakenly, to appease their greed.

The whole time he was busy focused on building a law-abiding legacy, Todd was just as busy expanding the criminal enterprise. The worst part was that Todd had the brains and clever sense to keep it quiet and his methods concealed from Rip and those loyal to him.

JD grimaced. As the group's sergeant-at-arms, he was third in rank. "How could you give it to those ungrateful, traitorous fools?" JD asked.

For so many years, Rip had been careful, not keeping

anyone too close because he couldn't afford any additional vulnerabilities. But last month Todd had taken his one weakness and exploited it anyway.

"Give me the clubhouse or I'll spill blood," Todd had said. *"And not just the Iron Warriors'. I won't waste a bullet on Ida. But you won't be around forever to protect the pretty little deputy, and once you're out of the picture, she'll pay the price."* A wicked grin pulled at his mouth. *"It won't be quick, and it won't be painless. Maybe a couple of guys will show her a 'good time' first."* He licked his lips.

Disgust swam through his veins as he recalled it. After Rip *showed* Todd what he thought of that proposal, with his fists, going so far as to break his nose, he'd given Burk the keys and signed the deed over to him.

"A building isn't worth bloodshed," Rip said.

Quill rolled his eyes, leaned back in a creaky chair and put a boot up on a table, kicking up dust. "Let those boys build their own place. Danger comes with the territory for us. If we get to hold on to what's ours, we can take whatever they dish out and give it right back."

They could.

Ashley couldn't.

She was smart and strong and a sharp deputy, but the badge wouldn't keep her safe. The depravity Todd was capable of, combined with his utter lack of respect for women—the guy even beat and cheated on his own old lady—meant he'd order some lowlifes under his thumb to hurt Ashley, bad, and then kill her. Not only to get to Rip but just for fun. "I don't want a war spilling over into town. Innocent people will suffer the consequences," he said.

"Are you talking about Ashley Russo?" JD asked, and all the other curious gazes in the room swung to Rip.

It was common knowledge that he'd watched over her

and ensured no Iron Warrior messed with her, but he'd kept it secret from Ashley how he managed to do that. Todd's vile threat only made Rip more determined to shield her. From everything, including herself.

"I am," he admitted. "But also, Ida. And your families. Once bullets start flying, bystanders could be hit."

Quill nodded. "You make a good point. The sheriff's department will only make things difficult for us, and cops are likely to die if Todd becomes so unhinged as to go after *your* deputy."

My deputy?

A part of him enjoyed the sound of that far too much. Ever since he'd seen her swimming in the lake with some friends, almost nineteen years old, climbing out of the water in a modest one piece, laughing, sparkling, radiating light, he'd considered how it would be if she was his.

The more pragmatic side of him was aware she didn't even like him and deserved much better than he could offer. So, he kept his distance and put Quill in charge of watching her, ensuring her safety with the full power of Ironside services at his disposal.

But the way she'd asked for his help, the imploring look on her face, the plea in her voice had been a sucker punch straight to his heart. That was the last conversation he'd wanted to have with Ashley. Upsetting her. Angering her. Disappointing her.

Denying the one request she'd ever made of him.

He'd almost caved. *Almost.* But helping her would not only go against the code but also meant allowing her to get in the middle of this war, which was exactly where he didn't want her. He needed to figure out her reckless plan and stop her before it was too late.

Her defiance last night, when he was only trying to keep her out of the line of fire, still had him bristling.

"This is going to come to a head, sooner rather than later," JD said. "There's only room for one club in this town."

An unfortunate truth. It was the reason Todd had called a vote to split the club instead of replacing Rip as president. This left those not loyal to Todd isolated and vulnerable to attack.

Todd was eventually going to try to kill him unless Rip got to him first.

"Rather than a full-frontal confrontation, there's a better way to handle this," Rip said. "Ironside is mine. They can't bring in cash through it without me. The authorities already shut down their prostitution ring." He'd had no idea women were being trafficked and pimped out in portable tiny homes that routinely changed locations. But Todd had at least three or four degrees of separation preventing law enforcement from charging him. "The only thing left is drugs."

"I heard he's expanding that," JD said. "He's got big plans."

Rip nodded, having caught wind of the same rumors. "And we need to know what they are."

"It'll turn out like every other attempt to get Todd." Quill heaved a loud, long sigh laced with weariness. "Teflon won't go to jail."

Since the cops could never make a charge stick to Todd, the club had given him the apt nickname "Teflon."

Rip also doubted the man would ever see the inside of a prison cell and wasn't counting on Todd's arrest as part of his plan. "He's most likely getting his drugs from a cartel. We need to figure out the inner workings of his operation and bring the hammer down. Find a way to seize a shipment. A big one that he can't recover from financially. One that puts him in the crosshairs of the cartel."

"So they take him out for us," JD said.

Rip nodded. A lot of moving parts to piece together to make it happen. But possible.

"That might work," Quill said.

Based on the expressions of the others, they weren't opposed to the idea, but they weren't sold on it either.

"How are we supposed to do that?" asked Saul, one of the skeptics.

"We start with a weak link. A little guy in the food chain," Rip said. "One of his dealers. Someone who will talk to us, but also someone we can rattle to keep quiet about sharing information. Any ideas who we can squeeze?"

JD snapped his fingers. "Yates. He acts tough, but it's smoke-and-mirrors. I'm telling you that dude will rat to save himself when it comes down to it. I think he might even do it just because he doesn't like Todd and the way he gets treated."

Burk didn't respect many of his brothers. That was why it had come as such a shock to Rip that so many had sided with him. Was it out of coercion? Fear? Bribery?

It certainly wasn't out of loyalty or love.

"But what if Yates doesn't know enough?" Quill asked. "Todd is a slippery snake. I'm sure none of the dealers will know everything we need to make this happen."

A safe bet that Rip wouldn't wager against. Getting information from one of the dealers was only a maneuver that would lead to another. Rip had already made a preemptive move before he'd given Todd the clubhouse. He'd left behind a parting gift. A voice-activated audio transmitter with a SIM card hidden in the room or rather the *chapel*, where they held *church*, their official club meetings. When its built-in sensor detected a sound over sixty decibels, it automatically dialed a preset number, Rip's primary burner phone. Then he could listen in. Thus far, he hadn't learned anything noteworthy, but at the same time, it also meant Todd wasn't aware of the bug.

"Yates isn't going to be the endgame guy," Rip said. "One step at a time. First, we find out what he knows, then we take it from there." His men nodded. "Something else I need you to do. Talk to the boys who we thought were loyal, who we never assumed might side with a drug dealer. Find out why they're wearing different patches now." At the moment, Todd outmanned them. Anything Rip could do to whittle down the numbers and spare some good people jail time, he would. "And be discreet."

Chapter Four

Ashley zoomed the telephoto lens in on the front of the Hellhound clubhouse. Ten bikes were out front. Over the past several hours that she'd been seated in an unmarked patrol SUV across the street, she'd snapped pictures of six members. None of them had a limp. But instinct told her to be patient.

Apparently, the ones inside, whom she hadn't seen, weren't early risers. Nearly noon and they hadn't shown their faces yet. She didn't know if any women were inside. Besides the Harleys, no other vehicles were parked out front. Not that there couldn't be some concealed in the adjacent four-bay garage.

They'd accepted a food delivery about an hour ago.

Why were they all holed up in there on a Saturday instead of at home with girlfriends, wives, their families? Half of them had kids.

Mustering together, getting their stories straight.

She looked around. There wasn't much traffic out here on Rock Grinder Lane. No homes or businesses in the desolate area on the far outskirts of town, aside from a couple of warehouses farther down the dirt road, a trucking company and a defunct cement plant. Other than a few 18-wheelers and vans that had passed earlier, there was plenty of privacy for the OMG.

The front door of the clubhouse swung open. Todd Burk sauntered outside smoking a cigarette, followed by three members of his crew. One was average height and medium build. Another was a heavy guy with a barrel-shaped torso. The last guy, bringing up the rear, was tall and had a distinct limp. Every time he put weight on his bad leg, he winced.

"Gotcha," she muttered to herself, snapping pictures of them talking.

Not that she had fingerprints, a detailed description of them to go on, or any evidence to link them to the attack last night on Rip. But those were the perpetrators.

Ashley only had to prove it. She took a couple more photos.

Todd patted the tall one on the back, saying something to him and the others. The three guys nodded as Todd turned, glancing around. His gaze landed on her.

She zoomed in for a close-up of his face.

He smiled, though there was nothing pleasant about it. His grin was pure evil. He gestured for the others to go back inside, then he jogged across the lot through the opening in the gate, and over toward her.

Stay away from Burk. Rip's voice rang in her head.

But she had kept her distance. Nothing she could do about the man crossing the street. She certainly wasn't going to speed off like she feared him. Even though she'd been afraid of the man since she was seventeen.

Ashley set the camera in the passenger's seat, started the SUV and lowered her window. Heart thrumming, she unfastened the strap on the holster at her hip with the flick of her thumb and rested her hand on the butt of her duty weapon.

Todd took one last drag from his cigarette and flicked it to the ground.

"That's littering," she said as he approached.

"Good afternoon to you, too, Deputy Russo. Feel free to write me a citation. I'd be happy to pay. I must admit I'm surprised to see you here."

Anger always overrode her fear when she saw him, but this was the first time they'd come face-to-face and spoken. "Someone broke into Rip Lockwood's trailer last night and attacked him. I'm here investigating. You wouldn't happen to know anything about that, would you?"

"No, ma'am. A break-in and assault. How unfortunate. The thought of a former brother under siege." He gave a mock shiver. "Terrifying. It's good the sheriff's department is investigating. But it looks like you're just taking pictures. Which is fine. I welcome it. Nothing to hide. In fact, I was counting on someone from your department swinging by today." Another vicious grin tugged at his mouth. "Just surprised that it's you." He let that dangle between them for a moment. "Want to come on over, ask us some questions inside *my* clubhouse?"

No way that was happening. "Why are you surprised it's me out here?"

"Well, your boyfriend paid a steep price to keep the devil away from you, but in spite of that, here you are, taking pictures, in front of the devil's house. Tempting him." He licked his lips. "Not wise. I bet Rip doesn't know you're here. He would not be happy." Todd shook his head as though reprimanding a child.

"What price did Rip pay?"

He raised his eyebrows. "You don't know?" A dark chuckle rolled from him. "Then I can't say. I don't want to be the one to spoil the surprise. But the gesture was grand. Undeniably romantic. You should ask your boyfriend."

Hearing Rip referred to as her *boyfriend* irked and in-

trigued her. Why on earth would Todd or anyone else for
that matter think such a thing?

"There's nothing personal between me and Rip," she said
flatly, not wanting him to see he'd struck a nerve.

A look of surprise and she dared guess possibly even de-
light swept over his expression. "You're not his old lady?"

"Old lady?" That was a serious term of endearment re-
served for a woman a biker was committed to. But there
was nothing romantic or sexual between her and Rip. No
ship of any kind. No relationship. No friendship. Nothing.

"Yeah. I get you wanting to keep it secret. You've both
got to keep up appearances with you wearing a badge. But
you can tell me. You two a thing?"

Something prickled through her, some kind of omen, at
him pressing the question, at him asking at all. If people
thought that, if the sheriff did, could it hurt her job, damage
her reputation? "Not that it's any of your business, but no."

Wicked satisfaction spread wider over his face.

She realized with a sinking sensation in the pit of her
stomach that she'd somehow made a mistake. But she'd
only been honest.

Todd drew closer, resting his forearm on the frame of
the open window.

She tightened her grip on her gun.

"You may not be intimate with your protector, but make
no mistake, it's personal. Rip really should remedy that
technicality." Todd sucked his teeth. "One never knows
how much time they've got. Life can be short. With the
slew of mishaps that he's endured recently, he probably
hears a phantom clock counting down in his head. *Tick.
Tock. Tick. Tock.*" He chuckled again, making her skin
crawl. "Are you sure you don't want to come in?" He hiked
a thumb over his shoulder at the clubhouse. "We make a

mean cup of coffee. Could probably scrounge up a Danish or a doughnut for you, too."

"Yeah, I'm sure. The boys will all say they don't know anything, the same as you. Their alibi will be that they were here at the club."

"Sounds about right." He winked at her, and it was all she could do not to wrap her hands around his throat and squeeze. "Suit yourself, Deputy. You drive safely back to the station, you hear?" He tapped on her door, jogged back across the street and slowed to a hurried stride, disappearing into the clubhouse.

Doing a U-turn, she rolled up the window and cranked the heat. She headed toward town, churning over everything Todd had said. A lot to unpack.

No doubt in her mind, Rip was in grave danger.

As much as she wanted her concern for him to be strictly related to the operation she was planning and the part she had hoped he'd play, it was hard to deny that it was also deeply…personal.

Hating that Todd Burk had been the one to make her face that uncomfortable truth, to feel it, she groaned.

She glanced in the rearview mirror. Through the dust on the dirt road that her tires kicked up, she spotted a black van behind her.

Todd had expected the sheriff's department. Probably to question his crew about last night. Whenever they were interviewed, they always told the same lies, as if reading from a script that Todd wrote. But the way he'd been looking forward to the arrival of law enforcement was concerning.

It niggled at her even more how strangely pleased it made Todd to learn she wasn't Rip's woman.

Ashley watched the black van speed up a bit. She told herself that it couldn't be anyone after her. Not in broad daylight while she was in a patrol vehicle. But still she sensed something was off. Just nerves after speaking with Todd, her brother's murderer, inches away from her face, taunting her. Given that she'd yearned so long for justice, and she finally had a chance to hurt the man that had killed Angelo, who could blame her?

Pressing down on the gas, Ashley drove a little faster, anxious to get off the barren strip of road and to reach the well-populated town center.

The van stayed back behind her some distance. She couldn't make out the driver, front passenger or license plate in the cloud of dust. What had made her think the person behind the wheel had been chasing her?

Todd hadn't threatened her, and after all, she'd only been taking pictures.

Still, she couldn't shake the unease curling through her midsection. She got on the radio. "This is Russo, who else is on patrol?" With her splitting her time and focus between the sheriff's department and the DEA, she couldn't remember.

"It's your favorite deputy," Mitch Cody replied.

He was a good guy and they got along well. "Where are you right now?"

"Black Elk Trail. Why? What's up?"

Not far from her. Only a few minutes away. "It's nothing. I'm on Rock Grinder, passing Cloverleaf now," she said, referring to the cluster of dirt roads named after boot spurs. "I was over at the Hellhounds clubhouse. Had a chat with Burk."

"I'm sure it was pleasant." His voice was laced with sarcasm.

"He invited me in for coffee and doughnuts."

"Ooh la la. Aren't you special."

As a matter of fact, she got the impression that she was, somehow, because of Rip, but not in a good way. "Anyhow, there's a black van behind me. I can't make out the plate. I don't think it's following me. Probably from the trucking company." But she wasn't sure and that was what troubled her. "It's silly, but something in my gut told me to check in."

The van sped up, closing the distance between them.

"Never ignore your gut." His tone sobered. "I'll head your way."

Ahead, the road made a sharp turn to the right and then back to the left. Only a little farther and Rock Grinder would connect with the wider, better-paved main street into town, which Mitch would turn onto any second.

Ashley came around the corner as the sun peeked through the clouds, shining over the landscape. She caught the glint of something up on the horizon ahead of her. Checking the van's distance behind her in the rearview mirror, she spotted a man lean out of the passenger's window, wearing a gaiter scarf pulled up over his nose, a second before she heard a loud distinctive crack—*a gunshot*—followed by another.

Both back tires on her patrol SUV blew.

Tightening her grip on the steering wheel, she fought to maintain control of the vehicle, but it was impossible. The rear end fishtailed, the tires skidding across the loose earth at the edge of the road. The SUV keeled hard to the right and rolled, sliding on its top before crashing into a tree in the ditch below the road, the passenger's-side window shattering on impact. The airbag deployed, making her cough from the dust particles released in the air.

Stunned, Ashley hung upside down, the seat belt cutting into her. The airbag was now hanging deflated in her face. For an instant, she couldn't move, couldn't breathe.

The sound of the other vehicle's engine roaring toward her fired her into action.

She hit the seat belt button, tumbling onto the headliner of the ceiling covered with pieces of the window. Glass shards cut into one palm. Aware the van had stopped, she drew her weapon and got back on the radio. "Shots fired. I repeat, shots fired. My tires were hit. My vehicle crashed in the dry ravine just before Nine-Point Star Trail. I'm in need of assistance. Suspects are still on the road."

Ashley fumbled for the door handle.

Jammed. The door wouldn't open.

If she crawled through the broken passenger's-side window that faced the road, it would leave her exposed to possible gunfire.

She aimed at the driver's window and pulled the trigger. Glass shattered.

The engine of the van revved and tires peeled off, screeching. She kicked away the remaining fragments of glass around the frame, scrambled out and got her bearings with her Glock at the ready.

Ashley ran up the incline, out of the ditch, and took aim. She fired two shots, one hitting the back door before the van turned onto the main road.

Sirens blared. Seconds later Mitch raced by in pursuit of Todd's thugs.

Drawing in a deep breath, she winced. Her ribs throbbed and her skull ached. She touched the wetness on her forehead and looked at her fingers. Blood.

Todd Burk had come after her.

Whatever protection Rip had provided over the years was gone and they were out of time.

Now, she needed to go after Burk. Tonight. There was no telling what might happen tomorrow.

PARKING AT THE crime scene at Fuller's Pharmacy, Ashley glanced around for the sheriff. She spotted Deputy Livingston suited up in protective clothing—white overalls with a hood, goggles, face mask, gloves and plastic overshoes—to prevent DNA cross contamination. Holding his kit, he headed inside. As she cut the engine, Sheriff Daniel Clark walked out of the pharmacy, tugging off his latex gloves.

Ashley climbed out of her truck. She was no longer woozy from the accident and the emergency room had cleared her for duty. No concussion and nothing broken. She ducked under the yellow police tape cordoning off the area in front of the drugstore.

"I heard about what happened," Sheriff Clark said. "Are you okay?" He gestured to the small bandage on her forehead.

"Only a scratch. It's fine."

"It's not fine," he said, his expression stern.

Of course, it wasn't. Deputy Mitch Cody had apprehended the driver and shooter. A couple of prospects, two young guys hoping to become full members of the Hellhounds.

"Did the perps talk?" he asked.

"They claim they didn't like the sheriff's department taking pictures and acted without any of the other Hellhounds' knowledge."

The sheriff pursed his lips. "And Burk? What did he have to say for himself?"

"According to Mitch, it was the same story. Burk even had the audacity to act horrified that potential members of his club would shoot at a cop."

"Do you think they went after you because of your association with Ripton Lockwood? Hurt him by hurting you?"

More likely to offend Rip than hurt him by going after

someone under his protection. It seemed like a leap, but then again Todd had a lot to say about Rip and the questions he'd asked her gave the impression he believed she was Rip's old lady. "Anything is possible."

"Regardless of the reason, I should've had you hand off this investigation to Cody first thing this morning. The MC has an issue with cops and an even bigger one with female cops."

Rip wasn't like that. He didn't have a problem with women in positions of power or authority, but when she'd joined the sheriff's department, he'd told her in no uncertain terms that he didn't care for her putting on the badge. Not because he disliked cops, but he didn't want her in harm's way, let alone pursuing the bad guys.

"Mitch has got it from here," she said.

"The Hellhounds and Todd Burk can't think they're going to get away with this. An attack on you is an attack on all of us. On the law itself. I'll pay them a visit later. Bring Cody and the fire department."

"Why the fire department?"

"Because I've got a sneaking suspicion that I'm going to smell smoke when I get there. Might have to bust through a few walls to make sure it's not electrical."

The sheriff was a good man and only wanted to look out for his people, but things were going to escalate. Todd's reign of terror was just getting started. The sooner he was dealt with the better for everyone. "What do you have inside?" she asked, wanting to change the subject.

"Homicide. Someone shot the pharmacist once in the head, twice in the chest and slit his throat."

"Unusual. Not what we typically see in a robbery." Perpetrators were normally in a rush to grab what they could and get away from the scene. "One in the head. Maybe in the chest. But not three bullets and a fatal knife wound."

"I think someone was sending a message," the sheriff said.

What kind of message and sent by whom? "Was it the father or the daughter?" Fuller's was the largest drugstore in town. Multigenerational, family owned and operated. Kind, decent people.

"Father. I need to track down the daughter to see what she knows. She was scheduled to work today. Looks like she logged in earlier on one of the computers, but there's been no sign of her."

Over his shoulder, Ashley watched the news station van along with the purple Jeep that belonged to journalist Erica Egan parking near the scene. "Media is here."

"I'm surprised it took them so long." The sheriff glanced behind him. "I better go speak with them. Did you need something? Shouldn't you be resting?"

No rest for the weary. Or the wicked. "The hospital cleared me. I just wanted you to know I'm going dark for the next couple of days."

"The DEA is sending you undercover?"

Debating again about whether to be forthright with the sheriff, she decided against it. "Something like that. The situation is urgent. A window is open. Now or never." She had jumped at the chance to be assigned as a liaison to the DEA's Rocky Mountain task force. Finally, she thought she'd be able to cut off Todd Burk's drug operation at the source. How naive she had been to assume the DEA cared about her small town or any of the others that Burk was poisoning. They had their own targets and objectives, and though she'd done plenty of good work with them, none of it had brought her any closer to her goal of stopping Burk.

So she was going undercover. Technically, she was still attached to the task force and working within the constructs of their mandate, but the DEA wasn't directly sending her. "I'm tracking down the drug supplier to the—" she caught herself from saying *the Iron Warriors*, the change was still surreal "—Hellhounds. I'll be out of pocket and unreachable until I'm done."

"Can you say where you're going?"

The less he knew the better for them both. In case things went awry, she didn't want any of this to blow back on him. Only her butt would be in a sling. "North."

"Tell Agent Welliver to keep you safe. I want my deputy back in one piece, preferably unharmed."

This went against her instincts, her training, her deep-seated desire to do things by the book, but drugs had now spread to the high school. Kids were getting addicted and dying younger and younger. Lives were at stake. Including Rip's and hers. This was bigger than the rules. It might be the only way to clean up the town and get rid of Todd Burk.

Just this once, she had to go rogue.

She gave the sheriff a measured smile. "I'll let you know as soon as I get back."

"You do that." He turned toward the media approaching the crime scene.

Her cell phone rang. Heading to her truck, she pulled it from her pocket and looked at the caller ID. The man must have a sixth sense. "Russo," she answered.

"Checking to see if you're squared away," Agent Welliver said. "Were you able to get Lockwood as an asset?"

"Not quite." She got into her truck out of the cold and started the engine.

"My recommendation is to keep working on him. I did a deep dive into Lockwood. No red flags other than his association with the motorcycle club. Honorable discharge from the military. Glowing performance reviews. His last commander said that Ripton was a man of focus, commitment and sheer will. He'll be your best way in and with his Special Forces background as a Marine Raider, you couldn't have a better person at your side."

She swallowed her bitter disappointment. It could take weeks to convince him to help her, and with Burk getting more hostile with each passing day, they were out of time. "If you could assign one of your agents to assist me for a couple of days—"

"We've been through this. The DEA is after big fish. Major dealers. Heavyweight gangs. Cartels. Not low-level dealers. The best I can do is pass along any intelligence to you that might be of interest."

According to one of Welliver's informants, a small motorcycle club in southern Wyoming, which had been narrowed down to her town, got their drugs from a pill mill—a place where bad doctors and clinics handed out prescription drugs like candy—and made their contact through someone known as LA, who was with another MC. The Sons of Chaos up in Bitterroot Gulch.

The town was outside of her jurisdiction as a deputy, but as a liaison of the task force, she had legal authority throughout the province of the Rocky Mountain Division of the DEA to investigate.

"Maybe the sheriff can get another deputy to help you," Welliver suggested.

They were short-staffed as it was, and Sheriff Clark was under the impression she was getting all the support she needed from the DEA. Her approach was thorny and not without great personal and professional risk, but necessary.

"That won't be possible," she said.

"Probably for the best anyway. You'll need a real biker with you to get anything out of the Sons. You need Lockwood."

Shaking her head, she slapped the steering wheel. "I've tried."

"Have I taught you nothing?" Welliver gave a dry chuckle. "Try harder."

The lessons she'd learned from him had been hard and ugly and most she wanted to forget. He operated in the gray, as she was doing now, all for the greater good. If she succeeded in this and needed DEA cover in explaining her actions, he'd provide it. If her op fell apart, then—

"You've mentioned that he feels protective of you. Something to do with the death of your brother. Exploit it. Better yet, sleep with him."

The suggestion was a complete blindside, leaving her stomach fluttering. First Burk, now Welliver. "What, sir?"

"If you do, I think you'll have him wrapped around your little finger."

"No, it wouldn't work." Not on Rip. He wouldn't take the bait. Even if she thought that he might, she'd never consider doing it.

"Might sound indecent but agents use a honey trap on occasion because it does work. If he's been protecting you from the Warriors all this time, then there's an emotional element that runs deeper than guilt or obligation. Trust me. If you get physical with him, the guy will do whatever you ask. I can practically guarantee he'll help."

"I can't."

Not that Rip was lacking in physical appeal. It was the exact opposite. Last night when he'd touched her, there had been something beneath the anger, a different kind of heat. No matter how hard she tried to convince herself the sparks had merely been a product of the argument mixed with adrenaline, she still wondered what his lips would feel like on hers.

Every time he'd visit, the rumble of his bike drawing closer, a thrill of anticipation went through her. After a while, she'd stopped feeling guilty about the way her pulse quickened when he came into sight. He had a way of pushing her buttons. Every single one of them. Gave her that strange, fluttery feeling with a look. Made her thighs tingle with simple innuendo. She'd always suspected he'd be an amazing lover. Once, after a couple of shots of tequila from the bottle he'd brought over, she'd been tempted to invite him to her bedroom for dirty, hot, pity sex, no strings attached, but then he'd addressed her as deputy, and the thought of Angelo and Burk—a man Rip viewed as his MC brother—had sobered her.

Why did Rip have to be a biker?

Then again, a dyed-in-the-wool biker was precisely what she needed right now.

Regardless of how much she wanted justice, she wouldn't trade her body, manipulate Rip using feminine wiles. Not that it would work anyway. Rip's charm could come across as flirtatious, but he wasn't attracted to her. Constantly reminding her she was nothing more to him than a deputy and an obligation.

"That's not a line I'm comfortable crossing," she added. "I won't operate that way. I'll find his pressure point and push."

But she already had, and it hadn't worked.

"Then Russo, you need to find an active *trigger* point. The difference being the latter is very painful. And make it hurt when you push. I'm talking excruciating. If your op turns up anything worth my while, let me know. Remember, you can't do this alone. To try would be suicide. Good luck." Welliver disconnected.

Ashley racked her brain over how to persuade Rip to do this without seducing him. Because that was not an option. He was against the dealing of drugs and had big reasons to take down Burk. Now more than ever. But working with a cop went against his MC code.

She had to give him a compelling justification to over-look that detail. Something he couldn't ignore. Something bigger than that code. Maybe she'd been too careful last night about not revealing her plan. He'd only help her if he understood the magnitude of the risk she was taking, the high degree of danger involved.

Being cagey like him got her nowhere.

The one thing she couldn't share quite yet was that Todd had sent his prospects after her. Telling Rip would only dis-tract him from the bigger picture. Knocking Todd's lights out would be temporary and would only provoke the devil to act more violently. The only real solution was putting an end to Burk's drug business and locking him up be-hind bars.

To do that, she would have to trust Rip. She needed to put the rest of her cards on the table with him and let the chips fall where they may.

She took out her phone and sent Rip a text message.

Your gun is cleared. I'll give it back. Meet me at Angelo's grave. Thirty minutes.

Chapter Five

Rip had a bad feeling about meeting the deputy, much less at her brother's grave. Yet, there he was, riding his Harley, headed for Millstone Cemetery.

Deep in his gut he knew she was still determined to carry out whatever plan she had, no matter how dangerous.

He was equally determined to keep her from painting a bull's-eye on her back.

Pulling up to the cemetery, he spotted Ashley's parked truck and something inside his chest clenched.

Chance had put him on a collision course with her seven years ago. Rip had heard about his brother's arrest, taken leave from the Marines and gone home to find out what happened. While there, Quill had told him about Angelo Russo. A first-year college student who had been in the wrong place at the wrong time and witnessed Todd trying to take advantage of a teenage girl. Todd had killed Angelo. Threatened the girl and her family into staying quiet. And had gotten rid of the gun tying him to the crime.

All speculation and deduction. Todd had only ever alluded to being responsible, at least to Rip.

Quill had insisted Rip go with him to the funeral to pay their respects to the family. At the time, he didn't understand why the older biker wanted him to go, but once there, he realized it had been an emotional ambush.

"YOUR FATHER ALWAYS *wanted you to be an Iron Warrior,"* Quill said.

"And I joined." *He'd wanted to wear a cut and ride a Harley since he was five, but the club didn't fulfill him the way he had imagined it would. Fantasy had been better than reality.*

"Only to leave. When you were meant to lead."

The Marines had given him an unexpected sense of purpose and belonging and family the MC never had. Just like Ida told him it would. "I'm on the career track." *He'd gotten great assignments, tough, but career-builders that put him in the fast lane for promotion.* "I was thinking about being a lifer."

A four-year enlistment had turned into ten. Why not make it a full twenty or more?

"A lifer?" *The dismay in Quill's voice was cutting.* "You made a vow to us first."

"I'm still an Iron Warrior. Wear my colors whenever I ride, no matter where I am in the world. When I'm here, I attend church," *he said, referring to their meetings.*

"Not good enough. Your leaving created a vacuum that Todd Burk has filled. The boy is a bad seed. Has sway like I've never seen before. If you had been here, in charge of the club instead of Larson, the way you were supposed to be, the way your father meant you to be, none of this would've happened. Your brother wouldn't be in jail along with those others. It was Todd who put them up to the robbery. And Angelo Russo wouldn't be dead,"* Quill said, the *words stabbing Rip like a hot knife to the gut.* "The only reason Burk felt so confident and cocky to kill that kid is because he's got a gang on his side. You never would've allowed that snake to wear the patch and get a choke hold on the MC by getting more filth like him to join. Todd is *running amok, getting worse every year, and will drag the club in a direction it was never intended to go by any of the founding members like me and your father. This is on you, Rip. You were selfish and ran away from your responsibility. There are many who'd still support you to take up the mantle. How many more brothers need to get locked up? How many more kids need to die before you take your place as president?"*

"Is it true? You could've prevented this?" a tiny female voice said as a teenage girl dressed in black, with dark brown hair in two long braids, stepped out from behind a tree. Her face was still damp, her cheeks flushed, her eyes swollen and red from crying during the service. Ashley Russo. *"It's your fault my brother's dead?"*

The men make the club. *He'd heard that a thousand times. The president guided the MC, but his real power resided in whom he did and didn't allow into the club. One devil could be like a cancer, spreading, eating away at what was healthy, slowly killing what was once good.*

The Iron Warriors always had a dark side, but didn't abide rape and didn't gun down teens. Quill and a few of the others had been grooming Rip to lead. Someone young, strong, principled, with fresh ideas, who would protect the moral constructs of the bylaws. But he'd never wanted the job, which they'd said made him perfect for it. And so, he'd run from the responsibility to lead.

Rip was an eerily excellent judge of character, the closest thing he had to a superpower, and never would've let someone like Todd Burk join if he had been president. The Iron Warriors were supposed to defend the town. Not decimate it.

As he stared at the girl, seeing the devastation in her eyes, the sorrow on her face, her pain called to him, and with his heart aching for her, he gave the only answer that he could. "Yes."

Her anguish flipped to anger. She stormed up to him and slapped him hard, her small palm making his cheek sting. "Then you should've been here!" She curled her hands into fists and beat his chest. "You should've stopped him!" Her screams were bloodcurdling, the sound resonating in his soul as she shouted and sobbed.

Quill moved to grab her, but Rip held out an arm, stopping him.

This innocent young woman was grieving and in anguish. She couldn't do this to Burk, but she could do it to Rip. And he let her.

Until her parents raced over, horrified. It took them both to haul the slip of a girl off him.

"I'm going to kill him!" she cried. "I'm going to kill Todd Burk!"

"Stay away from Burk," Rip said, his voice low and firm. "I'll take care of him."

"She didn't mean it," Mr. Russo said, his voice shaky with fear.

"I meant it!" the young woman spit out. "I'll kill!"

"Please don't let that animal hurt her." Mrs. Russo's face was awash in agony and alarm. "He's already taken our son. Don't let him take our daughter, too."

"I'll protect her." Rip took a tentative step toward them but stopped when the mother cringed and the father held up a hand in warning. "No Iron Warrior will hurt her. I swear it."

The girl's parents wrapped their arms around her and hurried away.

"How are you going to keep that promise?" Quill asked.

Rip turned to him. "I haven't signed my reenlistment

*contract yet." Something kept telling him to wait. To hold
off as long as possible. Most Marines had to sign twelve
months before their service date ended. Raiders could wait
up to six months, a special exception that no one talked
about, because of the stressors of the job. "Rustle up support for me in a vote as president. I've got a ton of leave
saved up. I'll be back as soon as I can. Until then, I want
the girl to be watched and protected. Make sure she stays
away from Todd and vice versa. Anyone who messes with
her, even looks at her wrong, they'll have to deal with me."*

RIP CAUGHT SIGHT of Ashley. She was kneeling at her brother's
grave, brushing leaves off the headstone. As he approached
her, he braced himself for yet another ambush.

He eased up alongside her. "I know why you asked me
to come here. Effective, I'll give you that." Being back at
Angelo's grave was a poignant kick to the gut. "But my answer will still be the same. I need you to trust that I have a
plan to take care of Burk." He'd told her he would handle it
and for too long he hadn't. But this time would be different.

Standing up, she gave him his gun.

His gaze flew to the bandage on her forehead. "What
happened to you?" he asked, erasing the distance between
them. "Are you all right?" He reached for her face, and she
jerked away.

"Car accident. This is nothing," she said, gesturing to
her head.

It took every drop of self-restraint not to reach for her
again and double-check she was okay. She stood there, staring him down with those expressive eyes, and he suspected
she'd only shoo him away once more if he tried.

To give himself something to do with his hands, he
tucked the gun into his ankle holster. "How did you get

into an accident?" She was proficient at everything. Always so serious and scrupulous. An excellent defensive driver.

"That's not what I want to discuss," she said. "You think you know why I asked you to come here, but you're wrong."

Silence fell between them. Not in a hurry to fill it, he waited for her spiel, steeling himself not to let whatever she had to say weaken his resolve.

Her face was stiff, her body tense, her obvious dislike of him palpable, which for some reason made him want to draw closer when he needed to stay as far away from her as possible.

"Once I leave the cemetery," she said, "I'm heading up to Bitterroot Gulch. Someone in the Sons of Chaos hooked Todd Burk up to his supplier. I'm going to find who and I'm going to cut off his drug operation at the source."

As she spoke it was like an invisible hand had reached into his chest and grabbed hold of his heart and squeezed. "You make it sound so simple."

"There's a difference between simple and easy. Regardless, it has to be done."

"The Sons are no joke." He knew those guys and was well acquainted with their president, Ben Stryker. Rip had a couple of things in common with the man. They were both prior military and tough as nails, but that was where the similarities ended. That gang wasn't to be trifled with. "You're playing with fire and you're going to get burned. If they find out you're a cop, they won't hesitate to do unspeakable things to you and then kill you."

She hiked her chin up at him, her expression so stubborn and her face so beautiful it hurt to look at her. "I guess I better not let them find out."

Scrappy as ever.

"You can't just walk in there and pretend with that group.

Have you even been trained for undercover work?" He seriously doubted it. She might be able to dress the part, but that was all. If by some miracle they didn't see beneath the facade she tried to put on, then they'd be entirely focused on her as a woman. Waves of dark brown hair and fiercely vibrant whiskey-colored eyes in a striking face that was a real gut check. Not to mention her body. Guaranteed to destroy a man. Heat prickled the back of his neck thinking about the way they'd look at her. They'd treat her like a biker groupie, though they had cruder terms, whose sole purpose was to slake the appetite of the guys. None of the above options was acceptable. "The Sons are a pack of animals. Those guys are a brutal, cutthroat bunch."

"That's why I need you. But since you refuse to help me, I'll have to do it alone."

Alone? "Sheriff Clark can't send you in there with no backup," he said, searching her face, and then saw the unthinkable.

She averted her gaze, a slight tilt of her head, as though hiding something, but also folded her arms, a defensive posture. He not only watched out for her, but he'd also studied her, knew her tells.

"He's not sending you, is he?"

"I'm on a task force with the DEA," she said, still not looking at him.

A chill slithered down his spine. "They most certainly wouldn't send you in alone."

"They go undercover alone all the time."

"It's what they're trained for. Not you."

"I can pull it off." But uncertainty flashed in her eyes.

"You're a lousy liar, Ash. You wouldn't even be able to bluff your way through a hand of poker with them. You can't seriously be thinking about trying to infiltrate the Sons of Chaos to get information. What are you playing at?"

"This isn't a game. And I'm done thinking about it. I'm doing it. Today."

"You're jumping into this too fast." She'd only first approached him about this yesterday.

"It has to be tonight," she said. "I can't afford to wait any longer."

"Why not?"

Averting her gaze again, she touched the bandage on her forehead. Then she caught herself and dropped her hand.

"How did you get into an accident?" he demanded.

"Work," she said, flatly, the one-word response not telling him a thing. "There's a window of opportunity with the Sons of Chaos. A Saturday night is my best chance. I'm going to do this."

Why was she rushing? "Hold off one week, and I'll give it serious consideration," he said, testing her. Considering and doing were not necessarily the same. A lot could happen in seven days to change her mind.

Her eyebrows drew together in contemplation that lasted a blink. "I can't wait that long. It has to be now."

"How about I call Sheriff Clark and see what he has to say about your plan?" he asked, not really thinking it through. He wouldn't jeopardize her job, but he also couldn't let her flirt with disaster.

Ashley whipped out her cell phone, pried off the back cover, and popped the battery out. "Go ahead." She shrugged. "The sheriff knows I've gone dark. And by the time you get him to believe you, president of the Iron Warriors, over me, his trusted deputy, which will take a while, it'll be too late."

Frustration burned at the back of his throat. What was she doing? "This is madness. I could call the Sons, tell them you're coming." Not that he had a number to simply dial, but if he dug, he might be able to get one.

"As you pointed out, they'll kill a cop. That's not the kind of call you'd make."

True. He'd never endanger her that way. "No matter how this shakes out, your job will be on the line if you try to go through with this."

Another shrug from her. "The only reason I ever put on the badge in the first place was to get Todd Burk. If I accomplish the goal, all will be forgiven. If I fail, the prospect of getting fired won't matter because my parents will have to bury me here—" she pointed to the empty plot beside her brother's "—next to Angelo."

She was willing to risk her badge and her life. "You would do that to your mother and father? They shouldn't have to bury another child."

Her eyes hardened. She was gearing up to be even more defiant, and in that moment, she reminded him of the innocent, reckless, daring-to-be-fearless girl who had slapped and punched him in this very cemetery. A different kind of man, a different kind of biker, would've made her pay for it. Might have even hit her back. But that wasn't him. All he had wanted back then was to take away her pain and keep her safe. The same as he did now.

"You would be the one doing it to them," she countered.

Too headstrong for her own good.

"You're asking me to break a vow," he said. "I'd give my life for you but that I won't do. Not even for you." If only she knew how much he'd already done and was willing to do on her behalf.

"I'm not asking you to break one. I'm asking you to keep two. You swore," she said, jabbing his chest with her finger, "justice for Angelo and to protect me. I'm asking you to keep both vows now. Or have you been stringing me along, simply placating me all this time?" Her words sucked the air right out of his lungs. "You can stay here and continue to do nothing besides offer platitudes and make empty promises. Or you can come with me. Help me. Not because I'm a deputy. Because I'm a sister seeking justice for her brother. A woman desperate to make her town safe again. Protect me, like you swore you'd do."

"I've been protecting you since you were seventeen." It hadn't been easy, especially once she became a law enforcement officer. The sacrifices he'd made, the scrutiny he'd been under. And now, no longer having the full might and force of his club behind him, with his chapter divided, could he still keep her safe while Todd remained unchecked? "Let me go instead of you. Stay here, out of unnecessary danger."

Her lips firmed. "Danger is everywhere. Closing in every day."

"For me, yeah. But you can stay away from it rather than throwing yourself headlong into it."

"For you *and* me," she said, and he wondered what she meant. "For the whole town. There's no hiding from it." She took a deep, shaky breath and let it out. "You think it's perfectly fine for you to go out and risk your life while there are different rules when it comes to me? I don't think so. This is my fight. I'm not sitting on the sidelines. Todd Burk has to pay for everything he's done. And I aim to be the person collecting."

The need for justice had driven her to become a cop, and he suspected it haunted her like a ghost, overshadowing every decision she made.

"Not just for my brother," she added, "but for everyone Burk has hurt or poisoned or killed. Get me through this with the Sons of Chaos and help me track down the supplier and, regardless of the outcome, any debt to me will be paid."

She was doing her best to box him in.

And he hated it.

She was a complication that he didn't need or want.

"Don't do this, Ash."

She eased forward, coming so close the tips of their boots touched, their bodies brushing. To a passerby, they probably looked like lovers, and that thought sent an ache through him.

Ashley tipped her head back, looking up at him. "Is there anything between us, besides your sense of responsibility?" She moistened her pink lips, and his gaze fell to her mouth and snagged there a moment. "Anything more?"

For him, plenty more.

Plenty that ran far deeper than he wanted her to know because she was off-limits. Every time his efforts at friendship with her had been met with skepticism or cool curiosity, a part of him was grateful he had failed to get closer. Because deep down when he paid her visits at her house, he no longer wanted to be confined to the kitchen and was ready to be invited into her bedroom. She stirred up his protective instincts as well as his desire. A powerful combination he was finding hard to resist.

But to tell her as much would give her ammunition to use against him and only a fool would do such a thing. "Anything more, like what?"

Stepping back, she lowered her head. "Never mind." She swallowed hard, her throat muscles jumping with the movement, and shoved her hair behind an ear. "I'm going with or without you. I'll follow this lead and put an end to Burk's drug trade, hitting him where it hurts, even if it's the last thing I ever do. The choice is yours, Rip. Whatever you decide, remember that you'll have to live with it." She marched off without giving him a chance to utter a response.

An icy breeze sliced through his jacket. He didn't mind the cold. In fact, he embraced the frosty wind. It helped cool off his temper so he could think straight. He had a lot to process.

Everything about this predicament grated. Ash going undercover. Rushing in. Unprepared. Unauthorized. With the Sons of Chaos. All alone.

His rule-abiding deputy was suddenly playing fast and loose with every rule in the book. And so help him, she was going to get herself killed.

Chapter Six

A tricky thing—not showing a hint of fear around those who could smell it, like sharks catching the scent of blood in the water. Even more challenging when it was the one emotion Ashley felt, second only to her resolve.

Being afraid did have the upside of keeping her mind sharp.

She sat sipping cola at the bar in Happy Jack's Roadhouse, doing her best to appear relaxed. In the mirror behind the shelves lined with alcohol, she looked over the twenty or so heavily muscled, tattooed bikers wearing leather vests with varying amounts of patches adorning them. Some wore hoodies or long-sleeved shirts under their cuts while a couple wore nothing at all despite the frigid temperature outside.

The Sons of Chaos owned the roadhouse—a seedy dive on the main floor with their private clubhouse upstairs—as well as the rinky-dink motel next door where she'd parked her truck in case she needed to make an inconspicuous getaway. The outlaw biker group used both businesses to launder money.

Two nights a week were open to the public. Thursdays were only for ladies looking to have the thrill of being with a biker. On Saturdays anyone, except for cops, was welcomed, making it the one night of the week she'd risk strolling in as long as she didn't have her badge. But she had gambled that she would also have Rip at her side and lost.

A flashing neon sign in front proclaiming Crime Happens Here had given her pause, but she'd still sauntered past the lined-up assortment of customized Harley Davidsons and hot rods into the roadhouse.

Inside, the place was crawling with bikers, their women, prospects. She'd spotted their president, a man they called Stryker, along with the vice president, but they were constantly surrounded by others. A couple dozen ordinary Joes and Janes were in the mix, playing pool, throwing darts, grabbing a bite to eat, dancing. Most of the women really should have been wearing more clothing than they had on. Attire ranged from sexy casual to downright skimpy. One even dared to prance around in cutoff shorts and cowboy boots. No way she was riding the back of a bike dressed like that in November.

To Ashley's surprise, more than a handful of women sported denim cuts that, on the back, read *Property Of* along with a man's name at the bottom.

The Iron Warriors had never considered any of the women they associated with or loved as property. And they had a policy of accepting any male prospect they deemed worthy regardless of skin color. A stark distinction from the Sons as she looked around, but they didn't seem to mind diversity among their groupies.

Feeling silly in her getup, Ashley kneaded the muscles in the back of her neck. Skinny jeans so tight she could barely breathe. Thigh-high boots. Backless, cropped, halter top. She was aiming to blend in and had overshot beyond her comfort level, going a tad too revealing. The problem was she had never had the wild, party phase. Her life since her brother's murder had all been about being prim and proper and then being a deputy. No parties. Hardly dating since guys seemed to lose interest after one dinner. She didn't really do makeup. And never did *this*—go to a bar and flirt with men to get information.

She wished she'd kept on her leather jacket after a big, brawny, hairy brute claimed the stool beside her and wouldn't stop trying to chat her up.

"Hotties don't pay for drinks." He leaned closer, his breath smelling of liquor and garlic. "Her next one is on us," he said to the bartender, who nodded.

"Thanks." She caught herself cringing ever so slightly in the mirror and forced herself to straighten and smile. "But I'm good."

He rested his massive hands flat on the bar top. Tattoos were inked on his blunt knuckles. From her vantage point, it took her several seconds to decipher what the upside-down letters spelled.

Lost. Soul.

Instead of *O*'s there were skulls.

She imagined how much damage those hands could do. Fists through walls and windows. Pounding flesh and cracking bone. The answer was a *lot* of damage. Not feasible taking him one-on-one, in the event things went awry. In spite of his relentless interest, this Neanderthal wasn't the right one to probe for information.

"Not much of a talker, are you?" he asked.

"Only when I have something to say."

He grinned, making the corded muscle of his inked neck flex. "I like the quiet ones." He put a meaty hand on her thigh. "Less talk. More action," he said, making her stomach twist.

The biker stroked her leg. His touch was worse than cobwebs across her face in a dark basement. She resisted the overwhelming urge to jerk away.

Picking up her drink, she spun 180 degrees on the stool, removing his hand discreetly. She looked around, trying to give him the message to move on. Her gaze kept darting to the door. Part of her clung to the unlikely possibility that Rip would walk into the roadhouse any second. She'd been in Bitterroot Gulch for over an hour. It took time to surveil the place, change into this ridiculous outfit and muster the courage to go inside.

Rip would've been there by now if he was coming.

She'd wanted to trust that his vow to protect her had been real. Not some hollow line. That when faced with the choice between keeping the MC's code and keeping his vow to her, he'd pick her in the end. To meet his responsibility to get rid of Burk head-on, so she no longer had a reason to hold any grudge against him.

A motorcycle growled up outside. A sliver of hope percolated in her chest. Seconds later, the door swung open.

Another biker waltzed in with his arm slung over the shoulder of a redhead.

Her heart dropped. It wasn't Rip.

I'd give my life for you.

That was what he'd told her, but Rip was a liar.

He always seemed to be there when she needed him. Flat tire on a dark road. He'd happened to ride by and changed it. As she was dropping off groceries at the soup kitchen, hands full, he'd appeared out of nowhere before a downpour started. Held an umbrella over her head and helped her carry the bags inside. The night she'd had too much to drink in a bar that never should've served her since she was underage, he'd snatched the car keys from her hand and taken her home. She'd come to expect Rip to be there, especially at a time like now.

If she was being honest with herself, it went much

deeper. She wanted to know he truly cared about her for some silly reason. Maybe because he'd spent so many years striking up casual chats that felt intensely intimate and got her to admit personal things, swinging by her house at night to make sure she was doing okay, giving her piercing looks that reached into her soul and heated her belly, trying to convince her he did care until she almost believed him.

She didn't want to simply be an obligation. She wanted to be a choice. For him to choose her. Not that any of it made sense.

Worse, she was such a fool for thinking the twisted bond they had ever meant anything.

"I'm Jimmy." The big scary biker turned around on his stool and rubbed the side of his leg against hers. "What's your name, sweetness?"

Why couldn't he take a hint? She crossed her legs, eradicating the contact. "Would you believe me if I said Sugar?"

"No, but I'm happy to call you whatever you want."

If this situation had the potential to turn into a brushfire, then this guy was gasoline.

Her plan had been to chat up one of the ladies affiliated with the club, get a feel for which Son to approach. But her stalker had been all over her the second she walked in.

Maybe if she didn't make any more eye contact with him, he would buzz off.

"Yo, Jimmy." A Son wearing a red bandanna tied around his head strutted up along the other side of her. "Can't you see she's not interested? Time to give someone else a crack at her."

Jimmy swore as he made a vulgar hand gesture.

The other guy laughed, not intimidated. "Leave her alone, man. I heard your old lady is on the way over. If she sees you talking to her, she'll cut this chick. And I kind of like her face the way it is."

"Me, too," Ashley said, shifting in her seat toward Red Bandanna. "Would love to keep it unblemished."

Swearing again, Jimmy got up and skulked off.

"Thanks for saving me from his old lady's switchblade," she said.

"She's not really coming. When he finds out, he'll be back. So you've got until then to sit on my lap and show me some gratitude," he said, and a sour taste coated her tongue. He called over to the bartender. "Give me a Coke like the lady."

Red Bandanna had been watching and listening. She wasn't sure if she should be flattered or concerned.

"No shots or a beer for you?" she asked, putting on a pleasant smile.

"Been clean for two years."

She swallowed a groan at having first drawn a scary creep and now the only sober guy in the place. Would he even have the information she needed?

"Congratulations." She set her glass down on the bar. "Excuse me, I need to use the bathroom."

What she really needed was to regroup.

She hopped off the stool, grabbing her purse and leaving her jacket. The restrooms were situated partway down a short, narrow hall. At the end of the dimly lit corridor, she spotted the neon red Exit sign. For a moment, she considered using it. Just pushing through the door and getting out of that place. But she'd come here to achieve an objective. Running from the Sons of Chaos and Bitterroot Gulch would only lead her home, where Todd was waiting. She had to stay and finish what she had set out to do.

Besides, on taking a closer look at the door, she saw a sign that read Emergencies Only, Alarm Will Ring.

Ashley shoved into the bathroom. Going to the sink, she opened her purse. Inside it, she flicked off the safety on her personal firearm. A Beretta, and beside it was another gift from Rip. A stun gun. She had the unsettling sense she might have to use one or both before the night was over.

Staring at her reflection in the mirror, she washed her hands. The rough bangs she'd cut herself to hide the gash on her forehead didn't look too bad. She pulled red lipstick from her purse and reapplied. That and some mascara was the extent of her makeup, and fortunately it had been enough to attract two bikers.

Only the wrong two.

She had to make the most of Red Bandanna. He might not know about the drug supplier, but he could find out for her. She just had to be more persuasive with him than she had been with Rip.

Ashley finished drying her hands and tossed the paper towels in the trash bin. She opened the door, leaving the bathroom, and ran into a wall of muscle and the stench of alcohol. "Jimmy."

Before he muttered anything, she rushed past him into the hall, making a beeline for the main area. The last thing she needed was for him to force her back into the restroom, where he'd have her cornered and she'd have to use her gun. The equivalent of pouring gasoline on the brushfire. All the Sons of Chaos would come running.

Her new objective was to get out of that hallway unscathed.

"Hey." In a few strides, Jimmy was in front of her with a hand planted on the wall, blocking her from taking another step. "My old lady isn't coming. We're free to have some fun."

She suspected they had very different definitions of *fun.* "I don't want any trouble. Just another drink at the bar."

Ducking under his arm, she scrambled to escape out of the narrow, dim corridor but didn't get far.

He wrapped his arms, thick as tree trunks, around her waist, hauled her to him and swung her around, pushing her back against the wall. "Let's go take a ride on my bike. What do you say?"

Her heart thundered in her ears and her body turned to lead. "Not interested."

"First time I ever met a *mama* who wasn't."

She always found the word odd used in such context, but uglier terms existed. "Maybe that's because I'm not a groupie."

He grabbed her bare arms, pinning her to the wall, and leaned closer. "Then why are you here, Sugar?"

The hairs on Ashley's neck pricked as fear washed over her. She'd have to roll the dice with Jimmy instead of Red Bandanna. "Drugs."

"Selling?" He cocked his head to the side. "Or buying?"

She raised her chin. "Buying."

"Why didn't you say so? I can hook you up." He pulled out a little baggie with a variety of pills, keeping a strong grip on her arm. "Name your pleasure."

"I'm looking for more than you can supply. A lot more. I heard LA is the one to talk to. Can you introduce me to him?"

"Him, huh?" Jimmy's eyebrows knitted together as he narrowed his eyes. "How about you pop a pill first to prove you're not a cop?"

She didn't let any fear show even though the emotion nearly suffocated her.

"How about you take your hand off her and back away!" a deep, familiar voice said, making her pulse spike.

A voice that haunted her dreams. Rough and husky. Dangerous as a blade.

Rip.

Ferocious energy pumped off him as he stormed down the hall toward them. His eyes blazed with fury.

He came.

Her heart did a somersault in her chest, relief surging in her veins. She'd never been happier to set eyes on him.

"Saw her first," Jimmy said. "You'll have to wait until I'm finished."

Four bikers hurried down the hall behind Rip. More Sons of Chaos.

Can't be good.

"I say you're done. Right now. You've got two choices." Rip stepped up to him until they were toe to toe. He was dressed all in black, only his patches adding pops of color. "Remove your hand or I break it."

Jimmy's gaze raked over Rip's cut under his sheepskin jacket. "I don't care if you're a Prez or not. This is the Sons' house."

"And this is my old lady," Rip ground out with a fierce intensity that sent a shiver through her.

Jimmy hesitated, eyes flaring wide, like the words had stunned him as much as they had her.

She understood enough about biker culture to know that it meant she was off-limits to everyone else, regardless of club association.

Jimmy dropped his hand as if it had been burned and then raised both palms. "She didn't say anything about having an old man."

Rip advanced on him, vibrating with rage, fists at his sides. Jimmy staggered backward.

One of the Sons clasped Rip on the shoulder. "Ease up, Rip, he didn't know," Stryker said. "Misplaced anger. Your old lady should've told us."

"Yeah, you're right." Rip whirled and shot her a look that could cut through steel. Those intense blue-gray eyes of his stayed locked onto her as he closed the distance between them in two quick, threatening strides, causing her stomach to go into freefall.

Her pulse beat wildly as she stood rooted to the spot, strangely transfixed.

He pointed a finger in her face, something he'd never done before. "Next time you make it clear you're mine." The rough and rumbly words made her skin tingle. "Better yet, listen to me and when I tell you *not* to do something…" He let his voice trail off, his gaze boring into her, and the longer the silence stretched on, the more her nerves tightened until she trembled. "Don't do it," he said, in a deep, throaty growl.

She opened her mouth to give him some argument, but her mind blanked. "Sorry, baby." The words slipped out in a whisper.

He brought his hands up, cupping her cheeks, tilted her face toward his, and claimed her lips with his own.

Rip was kissing her. And it was hot and unyielding and possessive. Not controlled and characteristic of his rigid discipline. Or anything like she imagined, and she had thought about it whenever she drew too close to him.

But this was different. He was kissing her like he was starving. Consuming her. Needed her more than his next breath.

His tongue plunged deeper, sliding against hers. All Ashley could do was surrender to the spark of heat that flashed into a blaze inside her. She threw her arms around his neck, coming up on the balls of her feet to better meet him, giving in to the passion and promise in the kiss that had her forgetting about their audience.

His hands moved to her hips, and he lifted her up from the floor into his arms. She wrapped her legs around him, confused how all the fury that had been blasting off him a second ago had erupted into this.

Him pressed against her, his fingers fisting in her hair, his strong arm looped around her, his hot mouth on hers, and desire she'd never known surged through her.

Then he ended the kiss as abruptly as he had started it. They were left gasping for air, chests heaving. She opened her eyes, meeting the most intense, heated stare in her life, and her breath caught.

"Why was she here without you?" Stryker asked.

A muscle flexed along Rip's jaw. "Give us a minute." He didn't take his gaze from her. "I need a word with my woman in private."

The sexual current running between her and Rip had her body humming with electricity.

"Yeah, all right." Stryker waved the Sons out of the hall, and they left.

Rip set her feet down on the floor and pressed his hands to the wall on either side of her face and brought his mouth to her ear. "Sorry about the little show we had to put on. We needed them to believe it."

The declaration quickly sobered her. Of course, he was just acting.

The man was good. A little too good. But they both did what they had to. No big deal. Meant nothing.

So, why did her heart sink?

"You all right?" he whispered, his breath warm on her skin. "Did that guy hurt you?"

"No. I'm fine. But I didn't think you'd come."

"I'll always come if you need me, Ash." His voice was

a sexy, rough rasp. He made her name sound sensual. As if it were a caress.

Rip stroked her cheek, a gentle brush of his knuckles across her skin, a reverence that erased her doubts about what he valued more—his commitment to the code or to her.

He meant his vow to protect her. Ida and Welliver had told her Rip had saved lives in the Marines, earning one of the highest military decorations. The hero. Rip had that complex in his soul. She only wished she'd realized sooner.

"I can't bear the thought of you getting hurt in this," he said. "So, my options were either kidnap you to keep you from going. Or help you so you didn't get yourself killed."

"You understand my job is dangerous." She kept her voice low.

"This is different. You're in my world." He sighed. "Listen, I know how much you hate me, but for us to get through this, we've got to pretend to be a hot and heavy couple." He pulled back and looked down into her face. "Can you do that?"

Rip thought she hated him?

Ashley met his gaze. "I'm pretty good at bluffing," she said with bravado she didn't feel. "I'll give them an Oscar-worthy performance."

"I'm going to have to touch you. If you recoil, can't sell it—"

"Answer one question. Did it feel real, the way I kissed you back?"

Chapter Seven

As real as the air he breathed.

She'd kissed him back with a wild hunger that set his blood on fire.

"Yeah, it did," Rip said, realizing it was all illusion. He could only imagine what a struggle that must have been for her while he'd been in pure heaven. Not taking into account the Sons of Chaos that had been standing around watching.

He'd been interested in women and thought he had a crush on Ashley. But holding her and kissing her, he'd come to the revelation that he *wanted* her.

Wanted her in a way that he shouldn't, in a way that he could never have.

His desire was supposed to stay buried, a burning ball of yearning and guilt and anger, deep in his core. Never allowed to surface, to be dealt with, but it stared him in the face now.

The low-cut, practically backless powder blue top she wore hugged her ample cleavage. The midriff exposed an enticing flat stomach but had given him the pleasure of feeling her silky soft skin. High-heeled boots accentuated the length and curves of her legs. He'd always had the impression of her being tall, though it was merely the way she carried herself. Not that she was short, but in the skimpy top and heels, with no gun on her hip, she seemed much less formidable than usual.

Vulnerable. That was the word.

She looked vulnerable. And the most beautiful thing he'd ever seen.

It had been an uncomfortable realization when he saw that Son towering over her, with his hands on her. Made his blood boil. Granted, Rip had been relieved that she wasn't tied up somewhere, bound and gagged, but still.

Every instinct that flared had been primal. Visceral. The need to protect her a fist in his throat.

But he had to find a balance between his concern for her, his genuine affection, his frightening hunger for her and the need to keep his emotions in check.

Rip didn't normally have an issue maintaining a handle on his temper. But he had come close to punching that Son in the face and knocking out his teeth. He couldn't afford to make a mistake like that. Not when it could cost either of their lives.

"But I caught you by surprise," he added. "Now you're going to be anticipating it. I don't want to creep you out."

"Jimmy creeps me out. Not you."

Now he knew the jerk's name. "That's small comfort."

"To set the record straight, I don't hate you, Rip. Tried to, but never succeeded. I've just been angry. Partly at you. Mostly at Burk. At the Iron Warriors. At the lack of justice. I hated myself more for not being able to put Burk behind bars myself than I ever hated you."

He caressed her face. "I can understand that, and I know pretending to be with me isn't helping. I wish there was another way, but there isn't now."

"Kissing you wasn't so bad." She bit her bottom lip and he wanted to claim her mouth again. "You're really rather good at it."

Pride swelled in his chest. It had been a while since he

had locked lips with anyone, but he'd never kissed a woman the way he'd just kissed her. Full of relief and hunger and an urgent need that overwhelmed him.

Ash put her palms on his arms and ran them up to his shoulders, bringing her body closer until her breasts pressed against his chest. "I won't have a problem acting like you're mine or selling it to them." Rising on her toes, she feathered a kiss on his lips, and he didn't want to notice how right or good she felt in his arms, nestled against his body. "Think they're buying it?" She gestured with a tilt of her head.

He glimpsed down the hall. Sure enough, they had a captive audience.

"So far, so good. Did you give them your name?" he asked, not sure what alias she might've used.

"Sugar."

He glared at her, and she shrugged. "What if they had demanded a name? Taken your wallet to check your ID?"

"Someone in the DEA got me an ID. Ashley Roberts."

Sighing, he gave a nod of approval that she'd planned for that. He knew she'd worked on a DEA task force, which required her to bounce between Cheyenne and Fort Collins, but had been unaware about the need for a fake ID.

"We need to get out there," he said. "Once again, sorry for how we'll have to play it. For the way I'll have to touch you. And for the things I might have to say." The Sons treated their women like property and would only respect him if he did the same. He'd have to swallow his disgust and get into the role.

"It has to be done." She cleared her throat. "This is important. When we get out there, should I apologize?"

"To them? Hell, no. But saying it to me in front of them was the right thing. Good call." He took her hand, and they started down the hall. "Follow my lead."

"Whatever you say, *baby*."

The endearment warmed his chest, despite being a part of the act.

Holding Ash's hand, Rip strode over to Stryker, who waited, seated at a table with his vice president and two other Sons. There was only one empty chair.

"She can wait over there with the other women." Stryker gestured across the room to the pool table where the scantily clad biker chicks had gathered.

Rip dropped into the chair and tugged Ash down onto his lap. "She stays where I can touch her." Just because the Sons wouldn't touch his *old lady* didn't mean the scowling women across the room wouldn't. Ashley could hold her own, but if they could avoid a brawl of any sort that would be best. "No worries. She knows when to be seen and not heard."

Leaning against him, she draped her legs across his lap and slid an arm over his shoulder.

Stryker cracked his knuckles. "If she were mine, I would've punished her in the hall instead of kissing her."

One of the dark things about the MC culture he always had difficulty with was how women were regarded as second-class citizens. The club was a means to an end for Rip, to safeguard Ash and deal with Burk, but with the Iron Warriors he didn't tolerate abuse in his presence. The one time Todd had tried to lay a hand on his girlfriend in the clubhouse, he'd put a stop to it and threatened to break his hand next time. *Property Of* cuts had never been acceptable in his club and he'd added to the bylaws that they never would. Some MCs encouraged cheating. He believed in loyalty. Not only among the men but also for the women who supported them.

"Well, she's not yours." Rip put a hand on her thigh and

curled an arm around her waist, tucking her closer. "And I don't like to damage what's mine." If he ever had the honor of being anything more to Ash than her protector, he'd cherish her every single day. "Can I talk to you without your boys?"

"Afraid not." Stryker shook his head. "Jimmy told us she's here looking for drugs. Didn't know you had a junkie on your hands. But it makes this club business."

Interesting. Rip hadn't anticipated that, and he'd considered a great many things before waltzing inside Happy Jack's.

It must have caught Ashley by surprise, too, based on the way she shifted in his lap, rubbing her soft curves against him, distracting him with her heat and sultry feminine scent.

A real relationship with her was out of the question, so he did his best to suppress his body's reaction. And failed.

He hoped she couldn't feel the way she aroused him, but there was no hiding it from her. What was wrong with him? How could the possibility of imminent bodily harm coupled with the friction from Ash against him cause such an intense physical reaction?

Must be the punch of adrenaline and the flare of hormones.

Rip reeled his thoughts in line despite the intimate way she stroked the back of his head with her fingers and pressed her lips to the side of his neck. "How is it club business?"

"Todd always griped about how you wouldn't let him deal." Stryker tipped his beer bottle up to this mouth. "You could go to him for what you need if it was just to get her high, but instead you allowed the matter to tear the Iron Warriors in two. Jimmy said she wants a supplier."

"*I* want a supplier," Rip clarified through clenched teeth. "Todd's. She was being overly eager, trying to find out for me." He rubbed his hand up and down her leg, stroking her thigh. "How does that make it a concern for the Sons?"

"We're getting to that." Stryker took another swig of beer. "Why the sudden interest in drugs? It's not your thing."

"But competition is. Todd wants to come for me and what's mine, so I'm coming for what's his."

With a sigh, Stryker set the bottle down. "Therein lies the problem. To connect you with his supplier is asking the Sons to take a side in your little civil war. Requires a vote, man."

His vice president leaned forward, resting his forearms on the table. "We could call a meeting upstairs, bring the matter to the table, but it'd be a waste of time. You won't have the numbers."

The Hellhounds had more support than the Iron Warriors. So much more in fact they were confident Rip didn't stand a chance of winning a vote.

He wanted to put a fist through the wall. "I need this," Rip said, considering a last-ditch play. Focusing on business and lining the pockets of the Sons might be enough to sway things. "I'll kick back five percent of my profits as thanks for making the connect."

"It still won't pass a vote," the VP said.

Since there never would be any profits, he could go up a bit, but if he ventured too high it would raise a red flag. "Okay, let's say ten percent."

Stryker stood, scraping his chair back across the wood floor. "We can't help you."

Ashley glanced at Rip, her eyes going wide in concern. But this discussion was finished.

Rip set her feet on the floor, shuffling her up as he stood.

He took her hand in his and squeezed, silently telling her to act cool about the setback.

Stryker walked around the table. "Sorry, man." He put a palm on Rip's shoulder and steered him toward the door. "If you'd come sooner, right after your club fell to pieces, I could've done more."

Sooner? How could a month have made a difference? Stryker was trying to tell him something, but what?

On the way out, Ashley grabbed her leather jacket from the back of a stool. If Rip hadn't been in the middle of Happy Jack's filled with Sons of Chaos, he would've helped her put it on. But chivalry was dead in that place.

Opening the front door, the Sons' president glanced over his shoulder and Rip did likewise. No one else was close by. As Rip passed him, crossing the threshold, Stryker said in a voice so low it was barely audible, "HT for ten."

Doubting Ashley had even heard the man, Rip gave one curt nod. Holding her hand, he went down the steps, practically pulling her along.

"We have to go back," she said in a harsh whisper.

The woman was going to be the death of him.

"Nope. Not happening." He hurried down past the bank of bikes to his. The Harley was in Ida's garage. Instead, he'd taken his Triumph Rocket. The motorcycle was sleek and powerful with ridiculous torque that hit the road like a berserker.

"We gave up too easily. We have to go back and try again."

Sometimes you need to know when to quit. "I know how badly you want this."

"Need this. It's the only way."

"We have to hold tight for ten like Stryker asked."

"When did he ask and what for?"

"Do you trust me?"

Ash didn't hesitate, she simply nodded.

He lifted her, seating her on his bike. "We need a reason to sit out here for a few minutes. Since neither of us smoke, we've got to keep up the ruse a little longer." Cupping her cheeks, he leaned in and kissed her.

The rush hit him again like water from a fire hose quenching the thirst of a man who'd been walking in the desert. Just as potent and intoxicating as before. Maybe even more so because when she wrapped her legs around his waist, holding him tighter, her fingers diving in his hair, rocking her pelvis against him, he groaned in her mouth.

Sure, they needed a plausible justification to hang around in the cold, but he would use any excuse for another make-out session, to hold her and treat her like she was really his. A taboo fantasy come to life. He'd always considered her off-limits, even after she grew into a woman and he'd seen her swimming that day, water glistening on her skin, shining bright as the sun, making everything inside him clench tight with need.

The world around him faded away, except for her and the possibilities he shouldn't be thinking about popping into his head. Of what he wanted with her if only he was someone else. Not some biker in an MC, fighting for his life. Not someone she was angry with and blamed for the delay in justice for her brother. Not someone a cop would be ashamed to be with. Not someone thirteen years older with his best years behind him.

If only.

He used those precious minutes. To imagine. To indulge in the feel of her lips and the warmth of her body pressed to his and the taste of her. To memorize the new carnal knowledge that would torture him later.

At the sound of approaching footsteps, a set of two, he pulled himself back, but stayed planted between her thighs. She blinked up at him, trembling, mouth slightly agape, dark eyes wide, uncertain.

Rip glanced over his shoulder. Stryker and his old lady were coming.

He looked back at Ash and ached to kiss her once more. Realizing this was probably his last chance, he took it. He dipped his head, catching her bottom lip between his teeth in a playful nibble, and kissed her again. Quick and hard. Then he eased away, helping her off the bike, and tugged her beside him. With his heart throbbing painfully from every twisted emotion those kisses had roused, he forced himself to focus on the business at hand.

"I'd tell you to grab a room at the motel, but it's wiser if you didn't stay the night," Stryker said. "You need to get your old lady a *Property Of* vest. Would've saved everyone some grief. Here's some patches."

The other woman offered Ash an envelope.

A fresh wave of anger rolled over Rip as he shook his head. "Not my style."

"Yeah, man, I'm aware," Stryker said. "You're too nice when you've got to be merciless. It's the reason you're losing the war at home. Trust me, you want it."

There was something more to the envelope. Rip nodded and Ash took it.

"Go grab us a room." Stryker smacked his woman's butt, and she hurried off toward the hotel, tottering on her high heels.

"What happened last month?" Rip asked, cutting to it.

"As soon as Todd formed the Hellhounds, he reached out to us. Asked to get patched over."

The news was a hard blow Rip didn't need. His heart

couldn't countenance the prospect. "He wants to turn the Hellhounds into a Sons of Chaos charter of Laramie and Bison Ridge?" That would give Todd powerful allies aligned with his interests, committed to supporting him in a war.

Stryker nodded. "He wants to roll you out, man. Only one club is going to survive in your neck of the woods. Todd has made a lot of friends here. After Thanksgiving, we're holding a vote with all the other charters on whether or not to let him join. I think it'll pass. That's why we can't officially assist you in your request."

Yeah, but he was sharing this information for a reason and not from the kindness of his dark heart. "And unofficially?"

"Unofficially, you're looking for LA. My sister, Lou-Ann," Stryker said, and Rip recalled one or two brief interactions with her. "She works for a dealer who operates a drug camp that runs a bunch of addicts. She used to pick up the junkies at a predesignated site, every two weeks, then drive them around for the day to various pharmacies filling scrips written by dirty docs. Big cities from Casper to Colorado Springs. Afterward, LA and the addicts would get flown to the camp, or the ranch as they like to call it, where they drop off all the pills, spend the night, and do it all over again the next day."

"Are you sure this is a major supplier? How much could they possibly get in a day?"

"LA told me that she brought in anywhere from 4,000 to 6,000 pills. A day. All controlled substances. Mostly opioids."

"That's major, but Todd is dealing more than that."

"Anything the dealer can't get with a scrip they get through a cartel."

Finally, a break. The lead they needed. "Can you give me her number?"

"I would, but she got promoted. Now she's at the ranch, managing distro. Out there, no cell phones and no guns for the workers, only for security."

Ashley put her hand on Rip's back, no doubt annoyed she had to stay silent, itching to voice the questions running through her mind.

Rip slid his arm around her waist. "Where's the ranch? Who runs it?"

"Don't know." Stryker shrugged. "Despite calling it a ranch, they're mobile and change locations every so often, but LA never discussed whereabouts or the owner. LA doesn't have loose lips. It's how she survives in that business."

"Then how do I find her?"

"Inside the envelope is the address of a pickup point. My guys would sometimes provide protection for her on the road, for the first day's run, making sure no one jacked her payload. She started by loading up a van with junkies at the pickup. Her runs always began on the weekend. Usually lasted two to three days. At night, they go to the drug camp. Give the workers food and their payment in pills. They like to do a big run before holidays, and Thanksgiving is in a few days. LA took off yesterday. Which means they're gearing up for processing. They either picked up some addicts earlier today or will tomorrow. You might get lucky if the pickup point is still active. Your best bet is to hang around there. Go as early as possible. Act like junkies looking to work for pills. If you make it to the ranch, tell my sister that Benji sent you." Rip raised an eyebrow, and Stryker added, "It's what she used to call me when we were kids. That'll let her know I really sent you. Maybe she can grease the wheels and help you cut a deal."

"You're sure that's Todd main supplier?" Rip asked.

"His only supplier. Everything he gets comes from those guys."

"I appreciate this, but what do you want for it?" Everything had a price.

"The ten percent you offered," Stryker said. "Only it comes straight to me. Not the Sons."

Greed wasn't enough for him to risk cutting out his club and going against their wishes. Presidents of an MC guided the club, they weren't dictators who ruled. Getting caught would result in severe consequences. "Why are you helping me?"

"I'm not helping you so much as I'm trying to hurt Todd. Earlier this year, at Sturgis, he got rough with some of LA's friends. One girl went missing. LA made the mistake of confronting him about it instead of coming to me first. He put his hands on her. Probably killed that friend of hers, too, who went MIA. If you mess with my little sister, you mess with me. Also, that dude can't be trusted. The way he stabbed you in the back and tore your club asunder." Stryker gave a low whistle. "I don't need that dirty fool wreaking havoc for me or the constant headache of worrying about when I'll get a knife in my back. If you can manage to crush him before the Sons vote on whether or not to patch his crew over, don't worry about the ten percent. We'll call it square."

"Thanks."

"Don't thank me yet. There are some Sons inside who don't much care for the way you operate. Letting her—" Stryker gestured with his chin to Ashley "—get away with that stunt she pulled, not making it known she was with you. That's something we would punish."

"Let me guess." Rip sighed, filled with frustration and exhaustion. "They also happen to be buddies of Todd."

"You got it. Look man, I have no beef with you. But some in the club already consider Todd to be an unofficial brother ahead of the vote. You're coming for his business. A righteous move in my opinion. But everyone knows the Iron Warriors are at their weakest. If you were full strength, it would be different, giving many a reason to pause. I suggest getting out of Bitterroot Gulch. Now. And expect some unfriendly company along the way."

Rip shook his hand.

"I'll do what I can to give you a head start," Stryker said. "Try talking them down. They think I'm out here schooling you about your lady. The fact that you 'accepted'—" he used air quotes, "—the *Property Of* patches might cool some heads."

Rip gave Ash a full-face helmet to put on while he grabbed the extra one that he had secured on top of an overnight bag with a pair of bungee cords to the back of his motorcycle. "Any time you can buy us would be good." Seconds, minutes, he'd take it.

Nodding, Stryker turned back toward the entrance of the roadhouse just as three bikers strode outside.

Rip shoved on his helmet and activated the two-way Bluetooth communication system. Grabbing his small overnight bag, he slipped the strap over his head, slinging it across his torso.

Ashley did likewise with her purse. "What about my truck?" she asked.

"Where is it?"

"Parked at the motel."

One red-faced hothead stormed around Stryker, but the president grabbed him by the arm as he continued to speak.

Rip got on his bike and cranked the engine, bringing it to life with a fierce growl. "Is your service weapon or badge inside your truck?"

"No. Left both at home." She climbed on behind him, resting her slim denim-clad thighs snug against the outside of his legs and fastened her arms tight around his waist.

"Then forget it. I'll send a tow truck to pick it up. I know a guy. We need to get out of here." He preferred together anyway, one ride. "Are you armed?"

"Always."

That was *his* deputy.

A pang of regret cut through him. What he wanted more than anything was for Ash to be his. But that was something that could never be.

He squashed the inconvenient desire and every distracting thought.

Because the one thing that mattered most was keeping her safe.

Chapter Eight

A cold knot settled at the base of Ashley's spine as they sped away from Happy Jack's Roadhouse.

She glanced over her shoulder and thought she saw people following them, but she couldn't tell if her tired brain mixed with the surge of adrenaline was playing tricks on her.

Rip raced down the long sleepy street as they headed for the highway and the relative safety of the open road.

"We'll get an hour or two away," he said in the helmet mic, over the comms system. "Get our bearings at a hotel and strategize how to handle the info Stryker gave us."

"Sounds good." The moment of calm gave her a chance to try and piece together what had just happened. "What does it mean if the Hellhounds become Sons of Chaos?" she asked. "Big picture."

"It would mean I'm out of time. It would mean added protection for Todd. That stopping him would be even harder. I can't believe how far out he's planned this."

"At least now we have a chance to hurt Todd by cutting off his supplier. Maybe even to goad him into doing something that the sheriff's department could nail him on."

"Yeah, but it's messy. Now I'm exposed no matter how this plays out."

"With Todd?"

"With everyone. Todd will know soon enough that I'm

going to come for him and how. They're going to mention you. If Todd tells the Sons that you're a cop, I don't know what the future will look like for me," he said.

The thought of this hurting Rip, upending his world, had the knot inside her coiling tighter. She wanted to save her hometown by stopping Todd Burk, not ruin Rip Lockwood's life in the process.

"Why didn't you listen to me and let me handle it?" he asked.

"Why didn't you just come with me to begin with?" she asked, throwing it back at him. "If we could've spoken to Stryker privately, this would've played out differently. His entire club wouldn't know."

"I needed to think. You only wanted to rush."

"Think about what?"

"How to help you without breaking a bylaw, the code," he said, and of course, he hadn't chosen her over the MC but had found a loophole. "Then I had to figure out exactly where you went. Once I connected the dots with it being a Saturday, only one place made sense."

"And what was the brilliant solution that kept you from breaking the code?"

"I called a vote to change it. With only five of us, the bind we're in with the Hellhounds, and considering my relationship with you, it passed, no problem. But it took time to make it happen."

"And what if it hadn't passed the vote?" Would he have abandoned her?

I'll always come for you if you need me, Ash.

Was that true?

She heard the growl of motorcycle engines roaring up behind them and turned to see flashes of yellow and black, three bikes coming up on their rear.

Gunfire erupted. One bullet pinged his bike.

"Should I shoot back?" She wasn't sure how the logistics of that would work. Firing behind her while holding on to him with only one arm.

"I'd prefer to outrun them," he said. "I'm going to need you to hold on tight. Wish you were wearing chaps."

Was he worried they might wipe out?

She stiffened against him, snapping her thighs securely around his as she tightened her arms on his waist. He cranked open the throttle and the bike exploded down the asphalt like a bullet.

The freezing wind whipped over them. The dashed lines in the middle of the road whizzed by so fast they almost appeared unbroken.

Her muscles twitched, aching to be released, needing to do something other than rely on Rip and his expertise in handling a motorcycle.

The length of black pavement separating them and the Sons in pursuit, who were shooting at them, continued to stretch.

"Fast bike," she said. "We're going to make it."

"Don't jinx us."

Too late.

A siren whined. Red-and-blue flashing lights appeared from the darkness and zoomed up behind them.

"They might be able to assist."

Rip didn't slow as they continued to fly down the road. "The Sons have got the police in their pockets around here. We're just as likely to catch a bullet from them as we are from a biker. Or worse, the cop stalls until they catch up to us."

The patrol cruiser wasn't far behind.

A train whistle blew.

Up ahead, the white crossing gate was already lowered

in front of his lane ahead of the train tracks. Yellow warning lights blinked. A train was coming, headlights ablaze.

He was going to try to outrun it and make the crossing.

She was all for taking chances, but one wrong maneuver, one miscalculation in the slightest, and ten thousand tons of steel would turn them into roadkill. "Rip, don't."

"We have to." His voice was steady, firm. "Don't let go."

What choice did she have? But could they clear the crossing in time?

The whistle blew again, reverberating in her bones. The long, high-speed freight train hurtled down the tracks, drawing closer to the crossing.

Twisting the throttle, he accelerated, and the bike surged even faster, the engine straining. Her stomach launched up into her throat as she clutched on to him for dear life, pressing the side of her head to his back.

The darkness, the rush of wind, pushed in on her, squeezing the air from her lungs. She dug her fingers into the thick leather of his jacket, hoping, trusting, praying.

He whipped across the dotted yellow line over into the lane for oncoming traffic and they rocketed around the crossing gate, barely zipping over the tracks—the glare from the freighter's headlights blinding—before the train roared by within inches of the rear tire.

The gust of the compression wave rocked them on the bike, the tail end swinging out. Rip slowed and rebalanced them and kept going.

Releasing the breath she'd been holding, she looked behind them. In between the train cars, she saw the police cruiser jerk to a halt, dust whipping into the air. The lights of three motorcycles pulled up alongside the vehicle.

A close call.

Deep down, she suspected there would be more to come.

IN THE MOTEL room off the interstate, Rip and Ashley had gone over the information Stryker had passed to them and strategized a flimsy plan to get to the drug camp. Start at the main initial point where the addicts waited to be picked up to make their rounds at pharmacies. With any luck, the location was still being used and tomorrow would be a pickup day.

"All the information I had to go on to get this far was intelligence from Agent Welliver with the DEA," Ashley said, seated next to him on the king-size bed. "He was in charge of the task force I'm technically still attached to. We should call him. See if he's willing to assist now that we know it's not just pills on the ranch."

"Worth a try."

The heat in the room had finally kicked in. He stripped off his jacket and MC cut. His cell phone rang. He dug it out of his pocket. "It's Quill," he said to Ash. "I'll put him on speaker. Just keep quiet. No more secrets or withholding information between us, okay?"

She nodded. "Agreed."

"Yeah," Rip answered.

"I spoke with the boys who we didn't expect to cross over to the dark side," Quill said.

"What reason did they give?" It could've been anything. Calling in political favors, backstabbing, bribery.

"It varied. Larger cut of the profits from Burk's new drug venture for two of them. But three guys weren't pleased with how you handled the situation."

Rip scratched at the stubble on his jaw. "What do you mean?"

"You tried to issue a decree of no drugs without taking a vote. They're upset that you didn't trust the system. Trust in them to have your back. Being a potentate who crushes the will of his people is being someone who destroys the backbone of an organization which you pledged to lead. A Prez must convince his members. Not coerce. Not decree."

Regret pooled in him. He'd been afraid to take a vote. And in acting out of fear, he'd created the very situation he hoped to avoid.

Ash put a hand on his leg. The concern in her eyes was a small comfort.

"They're right. I should've trusted them." Rip clenched his teeth and swallowed past the bitter lump in his throat. "Did anyone get info from Yates on what Todd's big new venture is?"

Quill sighed. "About that. Shane Yates is dead."

"How? When?"

"Sometime tonight. He replied to a text around seven thirty, agreeing to meet at the old clubhouse at nine, ready to spill details about Burk's operation. Never showed. JD swung by his place to check on him. The sheriff's department was there. Along with a detective from the Laramie PD. The Delaney chick. Crime scene tape was up. Wheeled a body bag out."

The sheriff's department and LPD? Seemed like overkill. "What's happening?" Rip asked, not really expecting an answer.

"No earthly idea, but the winds of change don't seem to be blowing in our favor. If I learn anything else, I'll call."

"I might be out of pocket and hard to reach the next day or two. If I am, don't worry about it. You'll eventually hear from me."

"Okay. Stay safe."

Disconnecting, Rip turned to Ash. "Can you find out what happened to Yates? He was one of Todd's dealers. We thought he'd be the weakest link to tap for information. He agrees to talk to us and then turns up dead. I don't like it."

"Sure. I'll pretend as though I'm checking in." She picked up the landline and called the sheriff's office. "Hey, Mitch. This is Ashley," she said over the speakerphone. "I'm out on assignment. Just checking in to say that I'm alive and well. What's going on in town? Anything new?"

"Everything is going to hell in a handbasket. Me and the sheriff went over to the Hellhounds hangout. Along with the fire department. Sheriff Clark tore through some walls with an axe. Burk seemed to get the point."

Rip slid Ash a curious glance and gestured for more information.

She shook her head and mouthed, *Nothing*.

Sounded the exact opposite of nothing to him. The sheriff was a levelheaded, cautious man. Rip thought he was well suited for the job and had even voted for him. Clark would never provoke anyone, least of all the Hellhounds, by busting holes in the wall of the clubhouse without good cause.

"Anything else?" she asked. "Any leads on the murder of the pharmacist?"

"No, but we've got another body. Two in one day. One of the Hellhounds. Shane Yates. Killed the same way as the pharmacist. One bullet in the head. Two in the chest. Throat cut. But it looks like the perp was in a hurry on the way out and dropped the knife used. Something to go on. LPD is bringing in Burk for questioning. Apparently, Yates was an informant for Detective Hannah Delaney. She's hot under the collar. I expect she'll hold Burk for as long as she can just to mess with him even if she can't dig up enough evidence for charges."

The police could hold him up to seventy-two hours before the prosecutor decided whether to charge him. The timing was a much-needed boon. The longer Burk was behind bars limited to making only one phone call the better.

The Sons of Chaos who had Todd's side in this war wouldn't be updating him on the events at Happy Jack's anytime soon. Rip only hoped it would be long enough for him and Ash to accomplish what they'd set out to do.

Once Todd learned about tonight's exploit, that he and Ashley were working together to bring him down, there was no getting around the fact that Rip would be left in a dangerous situation. Exposed. He'd have to make a tough choice.

One that was going to change his life forever.

Chapter Nine

Ashley paced near the landline on the bedside table. "You told me that if I found anything of interest to contact you," she said to Welliver, with Rip listening nearby. "Drugs from a cartel should catch your attention."

It was almost midnight, and the DEA agent was still in the office working. He had enviable stamina. A true workaholic. She knew getting assistance from him might take convincing, but she hadn't expected a flat-out *no*.

"Which cartel?" Agent Welliver asked.

"I don't know."

"How much product?"

"I don't know."

"Where's this supposed drug camp or ranch located?"

She raked a hand through her hair. "I. Don't. Know."

"I appreciate your eagerness and commitment in getting this far. Really, I do." Welliver sighed. "Once you have more for me to work with, we can speak again. But tell me one thing, did you go into Happy Jack's alone?"

She flicked a glance at Rip. He sat on the bed, hands clasped, resting his forearms on his thighs.

"No," she said. "I had help."

"How did you convince him to do it? Did you sleep with Lockwood?"

Her stomach twisted into a pretzel.

Rip's gaze flashed up to her. His brows pinched together.

She reached for the receiver to take the call off speaker. Rip lunged, snatching her wrist, stopping her. He shook his head. *Leave it on.* He mouthed the words at her, indicating he intended to listen.

"No, sir," she said, her cheeks heating. "I told you I wouldn't do that."

"Really?" The surprise in Welliver's voice was like nails on a chalkboard. "I don't know what kind of hold you've got on this guy, but whatever it is, it's worth gold."

She squeezed her eyes shut, bracing against the embarrassment. The sheer humiliation.

"Get yourself and Lockwood into this drug camp. Find out what you can."

Jerking her wrist free from Rip, she grabbed a water and turned away from him, not able to look him in the eye. "I'll ask him. No guarantee he's willing to go that far." Not after learning she treated him like an asset. *Thanks, Welliver.* "Worst case, I go in alone." She twisted off the top and drank from the bottle.

"If you're telling me that he waltzed into the Sons of Chaos den with you and got you that information, then I'm telling you this guy will go off a cliff for you."

She choked on the water going down her throat. Chancing a glance at Rip, she hated what she saw. He was glaring at her, jaw tight, lethal energy starting to simmer beneath the surface.

Ashley was going to be sick.

"I'm impressed," Welliver said. "Once this all shakes out, he might face serious blowback."

Now he points this out. How this would leave Rip *exposed*. She should've considered any potential consequences to Rip sooner instead of operating with blinders on, solely fixating on nailing Todd Burk.

"If there is fallout for him, what can we do for him?" she asked. "What are his options?"

"Not if but when. And short of disappearing? Not much."

Her jaw went slack. "What?" She looked up at Rip.

He turned his back to her and crossed the room.

"Yeah," Welliver said, casually, "that happens in situations such as these."

Her heart pounded in her chest, a sharp pulsating roar that filled her ears. "If this could burn him, destroy his life, why didn't you warn me of the repercussions? Give me a heads-up?"

"Look, kid, you've got a tough exterior, but inside you're soft. You've got a heart. I didn't think you'd have the stomach to go through with it if you knew. But don't beat yourself up over this. Lockwood was a Marine Raider for ten years. Trust me, that dude considered every conceivable risk before helping you," Welliver said, only making her gut twist harder. "Focus on finishing this. Complete the op. Find the drug camp. If you can confirm ties to a cartel or anything big enough for me to take more interest, then I can help you. Best I can do. Hey, Jasper is in the next office. We've got something in the works tonight, but he wanted to speak to you if you've got a minute. Says you haven't been returning his calls."

Just when she thought this conversation couldn't get any worse, it did. "No, um, I, um," she caught herself stuttering, "I'm too busy to talk to him."

"Yeah, I bet. You've got your hands full with Lockwood."

Rip plopped down onto the bed and dropped his head into his hands.

Her chest tightened. "I've got to go."

"You know how to reach me," Welliver said.

Ashley hung up. Slowly, she turned to Rip and stared at his back. "I didn't know," she said.

"Know what? That you'd blow my life apart with this?"

She went over to him and sat beside him. "If you realized that this could happen, why did you come?"

He jumped to his feet. "You dropped a bomb on me that you were going to the Sons and ran off! You left me no choice!" he ground out, and her head spun, her heart aching. "What am I to you? Just some asset?"

Hesitation tensed her shoulders. She opened her mouth but was at a loss for the right words. "I don't know what you are to me."

For a long time, she'd thought of him as the one to blame for Angelo's death, right along with Todd. Later, his actions had separated the two men. Rip had been kind and sort of flirty in his aloof way, always offering to be there for anything she needed. Their conversations redefined him into a would-be protector. But she never knew what was real and what he simply wanted her to believe.

She'd convinced him to help her with this, like an asset. Because she needed him.

But he was never something to be used and discarded.

Rip leaned against the wall, muscled arms crossed over his chest, jaw set hard.

He'd risked everything for her, going to lengths no one else had ever done. Kissed her and touched her and made her feel things she didn't think possible.

The primal attraction heating her blood now as she looked at him left her breathless. But she didn't know what box to put it in, what label to give him.

"Who's Jasper?" he asked.

The question knocked her farther off-kilter. "What?"

"Jasper."

"He's, um, a DEA agent I worked with on the task force." Answering shouldn't fluster her the way that it did, as though she had something to hide, but she didn't want to talk about the other guy. Think about the things she'd done with him that she wished she could do with Rip.

"That's what he is. Who is he to you?"

She lowered her head. "No one."

It shamed and confused her that more heat existed when she was in the same room with Rip, a guy she'd convinced herself for years she had to despise, than with any of her past dates, including Jasper Pearse.

"I've never lied to you," he said. "Have enough respect for me to be honest."

This shouldn't be so difficult to spit out but it felt like admitting to an affair when there was nothing between her and Rip. "Jasper and I slept together while working on the task force in Fort Collins."

No other man had ever followed up after a date, showing any eagerness to get to know her better. Other than Jasper. Her interest in him had been lackluster at best, but it was an opportunity to finally explore something romantic. Something sexual. It had been her first and only time being intimate with a man, but she'd felt more desire, more raw, hot need for Rip when he had his hands on her than she'd ever had for Jasper. No one but Rip had kissed her so thoroughly, so passionately that he had possibly ruined her for every other man out there.

Something about her attraction to Rip unnerved her. An attraction he couldn't possibly reciprocate.

"Are you two still together?" Rip asked.

She was startled by the odd undertone she could have sworn she heard in his voice.

Was he jealous?

What if all this time it was desire lurking beneath their arguments, the flirty banter, the endless tension and prying conversations that always got too personal?

That sudden thought seared into her brain like a brand, glowing red-hot and strangely urgent.

"No, we're not together. It was a brief, casual fling."

"How brief?"

"Why are you grilling me about an encounter with an agent, who I have no feelings for by the way, like some overprotective big brother?"

The color drained from his face as he grew still. Too still. Too quiet.

"We need to focus on Todd Burk," she said, redirecting the conversation. "We have to finish this. As soon as possible."

Staring at her, he said nothing. An emptiness fell over his eyes, the cool distance between them growing, spreading.

"There's something I haven't told you. About the car accident I had." She realized she was fidgeting with her hands and stopped. "Burk was behind it."

"What are you talking about?" His voice sounded hollow. Whatever numb mode he'd flipped into, he was still there, unsettling her. "He wouldn't hurt you, not until I'm out of the way."

Rip sounded so certain, but… "You're wrong."

"What am I missing, Ash?" His gaze sharpened, and he watched her far too closely. "What else haven't you told me?"

The harsh question came across like an accusation. One she deserved.

She'd deliberately hidden the circumstances surrounding her accident. Now there was no avoiding it. She had to tell him.

Ashley took a breath, steeling herself for how he might react. "I was taking pictures in front of the clubhouse. I think I found which three bikers attacked you. Anyway, Burk spotted me. He came over for a chat. Taunted me about some high price you paid. For me. To protect me. By the way, what was he referring to?"

"The reason I gave him the clubhouse," he said flatly, and she ached for how much he'd sacrificed. "Get on with what you were saying." His tone was ice-cold.

"Todd called the gesture romantic. I told him in no uncertain terms that there was nothing between us. Then he asked me point-blank if I was your old lady, which sounded preposterous."

Rip narrowed his eyes. "And you said?"

She stared at him like the answer was obvious. "The truth. That I wasn't. I left and then two prospects followed me, shot at me and ran me off the road."

Clenching his fists in front of his face, he shoved off the wall with panther-like grace. "I told you to stay away from him."

"And I did. Sort of. He approached me, not the other way around."

He stormed over to her, exuding masculine power, and she was strangely more comfortable with his anger than his silence. "The one safeguard, the biggest thing keeping you safe, you just stripped away. Like that." He snapped his fingers.

Seated on the bed, she tipped her head up at him. "How is that possible? What did I do?"

"After your brother's funeral, I had to go back to the Marines for a little while until my paperwork was processed. Do you remember an incident behind Delgado's?"

She thought back, combing through her memories, and came up short.

"You worked at the bar and grill part-time in high school," he said. "Went to throw out the trash. Spotted some Iron Warriors on their bikes. Decided to go over and make a scene. Threatened Todd."

Her shoulders sagged as she recalled. "Yes." It wasn't her proudest moment. She'd been in so much pain, the grief suffocating her, and then she'd seen Todd Burk and couldn't stop herself from venting her anguish.

"When you walked away and went back inside," Rip said, "Todd let it slip what he was going to do to you. Quill interceded, told Todd the only thing, the one thing that would stop him. The story he spun was that after the funeral, before I left, I was comforting you and fell for you. I staked my claim to you while I was home on leave…and that you were my old lady as far as the club was concerned."

She rocked back as though what he'd said had been a physical blow. "I don't understand." The words *my old lady* got caught in her mind and spun there. "Wouldn't I've had to know that I was your girlfriend, to pretend with you, like we did tonight, to pull that off?"

Letting out a heavy breath, he lowered his head. "Quill told everyone that it needed to stay quiet since you were only seventeen. When I came back to town, that explained why no one ever saw us together in public, except for us talking. As soon as you were of legal age, you joined the sheriff's department. Gave a different reason for us not to go public. They all think that you and I are together and that we want to keep it under wraps. Besides Quill."

Stunned, she sat there. "All this time, you've been lying about being with me?"

"I never asked Quill to lie or actually repeated it, but I perpetuated the story with my silence," he said, as though that made a difference. "Because it worked. Old ladies are off-limits. Period. The one rule Todd would respect until he eliminates me, but you've taken that away."

She reeled from the admission. "Wait. Help me wrap my head around this. For seven years, if I'm supposed to be your old lady, then you haven't had a real girlfriend or gotten serious about anyone?"

He shook his head. "No."

Narrowing her eyes at him, she found that hard to believe. "For seven years, *seven*, you haven't slept with anyone?"

"On occasion." He shrugged. "I'd go to Cheyenne. No one regular. Kept it discreet."

Oh my God. That was why he didn't have any female visitors at his trailer or sleep with women at the clubhouse. To add credence to the lie that they were together. In love. Committed.

"You can't collaborate with a cop, but you can sleep with one?"

"Yeah," he said with a reluctant nod. "There are clubs that have patches for a thing like that."

Gross. "Do you?"

"Of course not. I'd never brag or exploit you."

She believed him. He'd have too much honor to wear that kind of patch. But this story boggled her mind.

"What about me?" she asked, perplexed, trying to piece it all together. "I mean, how would you have explained it if I'd had a boyfriend." In high school, she'd been focused on getting good grades, graduating, taking it one day at a time without her brother, not dating. But once she'd started working as a deputy, she'd tried to build a full life. She wanted marriage, a family, thinking it might fill the hole inside.

"I figured I'd cross that bridge when I eventually came to it. But you haven't had a boyfriend, have you? Quill would've told me. Or you would've. Other than this *Jasper.*"

And she thought she would have shared it like she had countless other things, such as her awkward date with Dave, personal things about her family, things she'd never whispered to another soul.

But she hadn't. And Jasper had happened out of town. All the way down in Fort Collins. Where Rip and other Iron Warriors hadn't been watching.

The ugly truth of everything gelled and smacked her in the face. She leaped off the bed and strode over to him. "Are you the reason I haven't been able to date? That I haven't had a boyfriend? That after one dinner, every single guy, except for Jasper Pearse, seemingly lost interest in me?"

"How would I be the reason?"

"It's the only thing that makes sense. Has Quill been scaring them off? Have you?"

"What?" The denial on his face slowly shifted, realization dawning in his eyes. He shook his head like he didn't want to believe it and then took out his phone. Punched in a number. Put the call on speaker.

After the seventh ring, Quill answered, "What's up, Rip?" He sounded like he'd been roused from sleep. "Thought I wouldn't hear from you for a while."

"I'm going to ask you straight and you better answer straight. Have you been sabotaging Ashley's dates? Keeping men away from her?"

"Huh?" Quill asked with a yawn.

"Give it to me straight," Rip demanded.

"Well, yeah. Me and JD let it be known subtly. We

planted a rumor around town that you two were together. Word spread faster than pink eye among toddlers. That did half the work."

Ashley thought back to a couple of years ago when Mitch had joked that the reason he couldn't ask her out was because she had a biker for a boyfriend. She hadn't taken it seriously, thinking it was his way of letting her down easily. It wasn't the first time someone had made that kind of teasing remark, but she'd chalked it up to how Rip would stop and talk to her whenever and wherever in town while he didn't give anyone else from the sheriff's department or most civilians for that matter the time of day.

"When any guys went sniffing around her," Quill continued, "JD and I rode up on them. Told them to lose her number. If they pushed back, well, then JD got off his bike. Looked them in the eye and told them to stay away from her. Every time they caved."

She should have chosen stronger men.

But that would explain why Dave, a nice guy who shared her fondness for Mexican food, had literally run from her when she bumped into him at the post office and asked if he wanted to grab some tacos and margaritas a second time. Because he'd been scared off. By Rip's henchmen.

"You brought JD into this?" Rip asked.

"Had to. I'm not as intimidating as I used to be. He understands and can be trusted."

Rip's free hand clenched into a fist at his side. "I never told either of you to do something like that!"

"You asked me to watch out for her after you caught *feelings* and didn't want to be the one keeping tabs. It had to be done. Let's say she started dating, got into something serious, then the story that you two were together would've unraveled faster than a yo-yo and painted a target on her back. If Todd ever found out the truth, she wouldn't be safe. And you know it. I won't apologize for doing my job."

"Unbelievable," Rip snapped. "You should have told me."

"Don't ask, don't tell, right? You didn't ask about my methods, so I didn't feel obliged to tell. Figured it was best that way for both of us. Straight enough for you, brother?"

Rip stabbed the disconnect icon on his phone and huffed a breath. "I'm sorry, Ash. This is my fault. I set out to protect you and roped Quill into helping me. This wasn't how it was supposed to be done. I never should've let this happen, let them interfere in your life."

Shock didn't simply surge through her. That was too simple. A mix of everything did. Surprise. Fury. Betrayal. Confusion. It rose up, twisted together and turned into rage with one target. Him. "But you did." She could spit nails. "Todd sent his goons after me because I told him the truth. Because you didn't bother to let me in on the big lie. Instead of keeping this a secret from me, you could've talked to me about it and explained. Given me a choice, a say in the matter."

"Talk to you about it? It's not as though you've made it easy to look out for you. You never listen to me. Or do what I tell you. Taking pictures at the clubhouse. Chatting with Todd. Running off to the Sons of Chaos. And where am I? Here, with you, ready to jump off a cliff, apparently, while my life is about to be blown apart, because I'm too foolish to help myself."

"I didn't ask you to vow anything to me any more than you asked Ida to take you and your brother in." Maybe he would've been better off if he had never made any promises and stayed away from her. "Don't get me wrong, everything you said is valid. The bind you're in with the clubs because of what the Sons know is on me and I'm sorry for it. But do you have any idea how your actions, Quill's, have made me feel? How it's damaged me?"

Rip's brow furrowed. "Damaged you? I don't understand."

"I could never figure out why no one was interested in me. At first, I thought the hot guys were simply out of my league. I came to terms with reality, accepted that I wasn't beautiful, lowered my standards. Told myself that the only thing that mattered was if a guy treated me well. Not what he looked like. Not if he excited me. Or made me feel anything at all inside besides boredom. Because the problem had to be me. I needed to try harder. I went so far as to force myself to go out with someone I didn't even like, only to have him reject me, too." The gnawing emptiness inside her opened up, spreading through her. "For years, I've gone through that. Do you know what it does to a person?"

A sense of defeat eventually crowded out the desperation. Hope and the chance for love slowly withered.

Being with Jasper hadn't been better. Their time together had left her emptier than being alone, so why bother.

Holding her gaze, Rip stood frozen, but she didn't want to see the pain echoed in his expression as though he were the one wounded.

Chapter Ten

"Ash…" He shook his head. "You're beautiful." So beautiful it hurts. "You deserved the attention of every guy out there even though you were better than all of them. I didn't think about how that story might grow and get out of hand. The way it might affect you." Maybe a part of him hadn't wanted to think about it, to question why a woman as stunning and smart and spirited as Ash was single. Deep down, he'd been too relieved not to have to cross that bridge. Not yet anyway. How blind he'd been. "I never meant to hurt you. I didn't realize."

"Why would you? How would you know the consequences of that lie or the repercussions of maintaining it? How lonely I've been." Her voice broke right along with his heart. "How badly I've wanted to be touched. To be wanted." Tears welled in her eyes. "To have what everybody else does. Affection from someone who has my back in this world."

Rip had no idea of the depth of her pain, and she would never know how truly sorry he was that she'd suffered.

But he had her back, no matter the circumstance. If only he was capable of being a vigilante, he would have taken out Burk long ago. Instead, he'd tried to do things the right way, to see her brother's murderer serving time behind bars. But in waiting, in being patient, he'd unintentionally robbed her of something she'd needed. For her to think she lacked in any way tore him up.

Easing closer, he curled his hands around her shoulders. Her cinnamon-anise scent filled the space between them and worked its way into his senses, overriding his anger at the mess of things. He pulled her to him and lowered his mouth to hers.

Letting out a shocked gasp, Ash shoved him away. "Stop it. You don't have to do that. Keep putting on an act. Pretend to be attracted to me. Give me a pity kiss to make yourself feel better about destroying any chance I had at a love life for the past seven years."

An act?

Sure, he'd hidden how deep his feelings for her ran because she never seemed interested. Any attempts he made to flirt were met with a cool, almost confused reception, like they were speaking two different languages. Every positive thing about him he'd tried to share she'd dismissed, choosing instead to look for the negative. Perhaps she'd simply never believed any of the good things, including his attraction to her.

If so, he'd done them both a disservice. No more being subtle. Time to be blunt.

"I wasn't pretending." Rip sighed. "My feelings for you have never been fake. I know you've never liked me. I didn't mean to overstep just now, but it was killing me, listening to you think you weren't desirable. You have no idea how men look at you. Even in your uniform I see it." He scrubbed a hand over his face, tamping down the jealousy that flashed through him as he recalled it. "I've wanted you for a long time. Thought about what it would be like, us, together. As a real couple. You're all I think about. All I hope for."

Rocking back on her heels, Ashley swallowed like something was stuck in her throat. "The kiss wasn't just an act for you?"

"The kiss was necessary. We had to get through it at Happy Jack's with the Sons believing we were a couple, but I didn't have to get *that* into it. Multiple times. I used it as an excuse to do what I've longed to for a while because I'm attracted to you. Want you in the worst way." There, he'd said it. Put his cards on the table.

A ragged breath punched from her lips as if squeezed from her lungs. Silence descended. Her gaze wandered as she rested against the dresser. Loose strands of hair hid her face, but he didn't need to see her expression.

He was probably the last man she'd want and if by some chance that spark had been mutual, he had to consider his entire world was about to change. But he didn't want her to think he'd bail or that she owed him anything. "Our history, our current set of circumstances, complicates things. I want you to know that I'm going to help you see this op through to the end. No strings attached."

"Thank you." Ashley let out a low breath. "It's not that I've never liked you," she said, her voice soft. "I thought I couldn't trust the things you've told me, couldn't believe in the goodness I've seen in you." She looked up at him. "Until tonight. Everything you've done…wiped away the doubt that's been keeping me from accepting how I feel about you."

He eased toward her, hoping she felt as deeply for him as he did for her.

"You're a good guy, Rip. I wish I could've seen it sooner. Believed everything you showed me. I'm sorry I dragged you into this. I wish there could've been another way. I didn't mean to ruin your life where you might have to go into hiding."

"Sometimes stuff has to happen, I guess. Without the way things played out at Happy Jack's neither of us would've been as honest as we have. Found out the truth." He'd never regret getting the chance to hold her, kiss her, and imagine.

She studied his face. "What if the vote to change the by-laws of the Iron Warriors to work with a cop hadn't gone in your favor?"

"The odds were pretty good, but I'd be here anyway. I would've waited until after we finished doing whatever is necessary to end this thing with Burk before I stripped off my patches and walked away from the club." He was prepared to give it all up.

"Really? For me?"

"This thing between us started out as an obligation I took upon myself. I'm not sure what it's become. All I know is that I'd do anything for you. The affection I have for you is real, and I want you in a way I've never wanted another woman."

Ashley pressed her palms to his chest. "I want you, too. Kind of scares me how much." She curled one warm hand around his arm and slid the other over the back of his neck. Her fingers stroked his hair, enticing him to soften.

But he couldn't ignore the uncertainty in her eyes. He no longer doubted that she wanted to sleep with him, but how did she feel about him?

"What am I to you?" he asked.

She was quiet, that beautiful gaze of hers stark. Perhaps she was surprised that he persisted in raising the question but also once more considering an answer. Then she looked away.

Again, she didn't know.

Not that he blamed her. First, she was angry at him and now she wasn't. Had questioned his character and now trusted in him without hesitation. Denied her attraction to him and now wanted to explore it.

But bikers and cops didn't mix.

Not to mention they were in different places in their lives. There would be fallout from his actions tonight. Once he rid his town of Todd Burk, one way or another, he'd have to leave before the Sons of Chaos came after him for payback.

"This isn't a game for me," he said.

"For me either." Lifting onto the balls of her feet, she leaned in, her mouth reaching toward his.

Rip locked down every muscle in his body and pulled his head back. "I won't be satisfied with one night." He stepped to the side, crossing the room. "With a brief, casual fling like you had with Jasper." The thought of that guy, any guy, touching her burned a hole in him. "I'd want more." A lot more. More than he had a right to have. Not simply rough, hot pleasure in a dark hotel room. The elusive more of a connection that was physical and emotional and serious.

"You don't understand. Jasper was convenient and he was interested," she said, as though that made things better.

"I'm convenient and clearly interested." A convenient asset, who could no longer hide his attraction to her.

Pressing a palm to her forehead, she lowered her gaze. "I slept with him because I didn't want to be a virgin anymore, okay?" Her voice was low, embarrassed. "But I didn't feel anything for him. That's why it was a meaningless fling." She looked up at him. "But this, us, it feels different."

Jasper was her first lover. Jealousy tangled with guilt and coiled within Rip. She'd simply given her virginity to the first yahoo who made it to a second date. Had a meaningless experience because she'd been denied the ability to have anything else.

He wanted to punch Quill and then himself for boxing her into that position.

"It wouldn't be fair to ask you for what I want." Even if she could give it. "The way I allowed Quill to handle things prevented you from dating and playing the field." Though Rip hadn't realized such horrible interference was happening, ultimately, the responsibility fell on his shoulders. "I won't take that away from you anymore. I'm thirty-eight. Doesn't feel old to me, but I'm already graying, and I've sown my wild oats. I know what I want. Who I want." Even if he didn't deserve her. "I can't undo my mistakes, but I can give you time. Without me or the club hovering, sabotaging your efforts to find what you've been looking for. Once we get Todd, put an end to him and I fix what I broke in the club, my obligation will be done. I'll move on from Laramie. And you can be free."

She blinked, her eyes filling with hurt, surprise slackening her features.

He didn't have time to choose his words carefully because if she kissed him again, he'd break apart and cave.

Rip snatched his jacket and helmet. "I'm going to run to that big twenty-four convenience store at the rest area we passed on the interstate. Get you some things for tomorrow. Sweatshirt. Sneakers. I've got an extra toothbrush in my overnight bag and you can sleep in one of my T-shirts. Don't wait up for me."

He left the room, shutting the door behind him.

Getting on his bike, he wrestled with his feelings. He wanted to make love to her more than anything, but she was special and deserved a man who would be serious about her. Who would be able to stick around and give her everything. To be everything for her.

Once some lines were crossed, there was no going back.

No doubt in his mind what she meant to him. He'd sacrifice everything, including his own desires, to make sure she got the chance to have the life she deserved.

ASHLEY CONSIDERED GOING after him but had no idea what to say.

What am I to you?

Because she didn't have an answer, he was prepared to push her away for good.

Something banded around her lungs, tight and squeezing. A depth and breadth of emotions she'd need time to sort through.

The secrets, the feelings they'd each unloaded were big and powerful and overwhelming.

She unzipped his bag, got toiletries and a T-shirt. A long shower gave her a chance to process, think, unwind. The water poured down on her, too hot, pricking her skin, but Ashley didn't care. When she toweled off, anxiety hadn't subsided, and putting on Rip's T-shirt didn't make it better. She climbed into the bed under the covers.

Sleep was impossible. She lay in bed, adrift and uncertain. Her life was caught in a whirlwind. This was the eye of the storm. The quiet, the calm, before more pieces of their lives got ripped away, changed forever.

Unease ticked through her over how Rip had left things. He'd been in her life, protecting her for seven years, letting his feelings for her grow, slow and steady and sure. But for her a cork had popped on the mix of emotions she'd kept bottled inside. Gushing and fizzing, overflowing into a mess.

Now he wanted her to simply contain it because circumstances made it inconvenient.

That part was unfair.

She stared at the red digital numbers on the clock. It wasn't until after two in the morning when she heard the purr of Rip's bike pull up outside.

He tiptoed into the room, not making a sound with the shopping bags, closing the door with a soft click.

"You don't have to be quiet. I'm not asleep." She sat up, bringing her knees to her chest under the covers and wrapping her arms around her legs.

He set the bags down on the floor. "You need to get some rest."

"We both do. But I need to talk to you first."

"You don't have to say anything."

"I do." She sighed, wanting to take her fizzy feelings and pour them into a neat glass he'd understand. "There are three phone numbers that I have memorized and know by heart. The landline to my parents' house, the sheriff's office and your cell phone."

"What does that have to do with anything?"

That was everything. He was one of the most important people in her life and she was only now realizing it.

"I don't know what you are to me because I never gave myself a chance to unpack it. During all the time we've spent together, throughout every conversation, every quick meal at my house, I've doubted you. While you were getting to know me, sharing who you really were, I refused to believe anything you told me was honest. Real. Until Ida and Welliver convinced me I should be looking at you differently." She released a heavy breath. "Whenever you're within arm's reach, I've been drawn to you, always tempted to get closer, daring to do so, curious to see what might happen, despite the fact you seemed determined to keep your distance. I tried to deny how attracted I am to you, constantly fighting against it. Told myself that it was just oxytocin, dopamine, norepinephrine. A chemical reaction in my brain that I couldn't trust."

Crossing his arms, he leaned against the wall. "The whole universe is a chemical reaction. But it's still real."

"You're right, and tonight changed everything."

"How so?"

"For one thing, you proved to me you're committed to stopping Burk. But there's more." She went to get up.

But he raised a palm, warding her off. "Stay there. Under the covers. Please."

"Then you come closer. Sit by me."

Rip hesitated a moment and then eased across the room and sat on the edge of the bed near her feet.

"Jasper gave me attention. Pursued me. I liked it and thought that meant I wanted him. But I was wrong. On my dates with him, I found my mind veering to you. Wasn't sure why. Sex with him—"

"I don't want to know." He hung his head and clasped his hands.

"It'd been fine. Nothing thrilling. Or sweet. Or special. But tonight, with you, was all that and so much more when you touched me and kissed me." Fireworks went off inside her body. "It was like my heart was beating so hard it was going to come straight out my chest. You made me ache, Rip, with real desire." She'd never experienced a hollow sensation between her thighs akin to pain. Never felt like she might die if she didn't get a man's hands all over her body. Not until him. "I don't want to fight what I feel for you anymore."

She crawled out from under the covers and climbed onto

his lap, settling her knees on either side of his thighs. Staring into his eyes, she slid her palms up his chest and then to his shoulders.

Rip stiffened while everything inside her eased. "Ash, please don't. You need to be free of me. Free of Todd. Free to see what your life could be without the pressure of this weighing on you."

Sometimes high pressure and intense heat were necessary to forge something new.

"I don't know what you are to me, but I need to figure it out." Despite the undercurrent of confusion, the suddenness of the tide washing away false beliefs, she couldn't ignore the truth that being close to him, like this, felt right. Absolutely right. Him. Here. The two of them. "What I do know is that you make me want to take off my clothes and throw caution to the wind and forget about every rule, Rip." She pulled the T-shirt over her head and let it hit the floor, exposing her body to him.

A harsh, shuddering breath rushed from his mouth as his gaze fell over her. "You need time. A chance to find someone, anyone else. Not me taking advantage of you. I promised myself that I wouldn't do this. That I wouldn't make love to you. Told myself that I wouldn't even take off my pants when I got back to the room."

Smiling, she cupped his handsome face and caressed his cheeks. He was an honorable man. Strong, fierce Rip, with his rugged good looks, cropped hair, stormy blue-gray eyes and that golden skin. Such a good guy, but right now, she wanted him to be bad in the best way. "Touch me. Hold me. Talk to me about all the things you've been trying to share but I've been too stubborn to hear. And if it makes you feel any better, I'm not asking you to break a promise to yourself. You can keep your pants on. But at least let me take your shirt off."

She pushed his leather jacket back from his shoulders. Tugged his arms from the sleeves. Stripped off his Henley. All hard-packed, well-honed muscle, without an ounce of fat. She slid her arms around his neck, pressing her body to his, skin to skin, melting into his warmth. His pulse raced beneath her touch as he stiffened.

"You and I are an impossibility." His somber tone tugged at her heart. "Where do you think this could go from here?"

"I don't know, but don't draw a hard line. Not when the sand around us keeps shifting. This thing between us runs deeper than anything I've ever known. Give me a chance to understand it. To fully feel it."

His piercing gaze was unwavering on hers. The awareness between them, the raw attraction, finally acknowledged, vibrated like sparks in the air, crackling with a new kind of electricity.

She brushed her lips over his and she trembled, or he did. Maybe both of them.

His jaw tightened, and still, he didn't put a finger on her.

Her heart couldn't take another rejection. Not from him. Not when she'd never wanted anyone more.

"Please, Rip," she said, filling her voice with every drop of desire running through her.

He looped an arm around her waist, cradled her cheek in one of his hands and stared at her like he was deliberating.

So, she slid her mouth against his and kissed him, insistent, determined, rocking her hips over the bulge in his jeans. Need twisted deep inside her. She yearned to explore his body until every contour was etched in her bones. No matter what happened tomorrow, or next week, she'd at least have that and this feeling.

Alive.

Electric.

Connected.

She clung to him. Pushing against him as if she could push herself all the way *into* him. Her pulse was a hammer, hard and resilient, thundering out a message—*don't let go, don't let go, don't let go.*

And finally, he kissed her back, his tongue sweeping over hers, delving deeper, drinking her in, erasing any questions or concerns, leaving only the powerful feelings she had for him. And in his arms, it was all that mattered. It was everything.

Chapter Eleven

The truth had a way of surfacing, regardless if it was convenient. The honesty Rip and Ash had disclosed changed things between them, for better or worse.

But redrawing physical boundaries complicated everything.

Rip sat behind the steering wheel of Ash's vehicle. The tow truck had dropped it off before sunrise and the driver had collected his bike, agreeing to take it on to Laramie for a steep fee. Then they drove to the address in Casper listed on the paper Stryker had given them. To a transport hub where they'd been waiting three hours.

Looking through binoculars, he stared out the windshield, staying vigilant, forcing himself not to look at Ash asleep in the passenger's seat, trying not to replay last night in his head. She'd taken off the T-shirt and had nothing underneath. All those soft, supple curves more beautiful than he'd imagined. Her killer body perfect to him. Sexy Ash.

Gutsy Ash.

Off-limits Ash.

Or at least she had been in some ways, but in one very important way to him she still was.

She had no idea how badly he wanted her. He'd tried to do the right thing, the noble thing, and he'd given her what he could. Kisses. Comfort. Tenderness. Pleasure again and again, with his fingers and his mouth, touching and tasting, and he'd reveled in her sweet cries of satisfaction. Then she'd asked for more, for him to be inside her. Need roared up like a wild beast, clawing through him, and he ached to have her. If he'd had protection in his wallet or had bought some at the store, he might've been a weaker man, but instead he kept his pants on as promised.

Ashley had been robbed of so much, he just wanted to give, not take.

Making love to her when he only had to leave later would've torn something from him. Something deep he didn't think he'd ever get back.

A part of his soul.

After the Marines and the club, he didn't have all that many pieces left.

Across the street, a small group of desperados had formed at the far end of the hub at the last bus shelter. Only seven. Every one of them had the anxious, fidgety vibe of an addict. Two looked as though they hadn't changed their clothes or showered in a few days and held a trash bag, partially full of items. The others had knapsacks, and one woman carried a huge tote capable of holding almost anything. They all appeared to be in rough shape.

With no one else around, they also stood out.

"Hey." Rip caressed her face with the back of his hand, brushing his knuckles across her cheek. "Time to get up." He hated to disturb her and wished he could've risked her sleeping longer.

Ashley stirred. Yawning, she stretched.

He took a small vial of peppermint oil he purchased from the store out of his pocket and applied a drop near the corner of each eye.

"What's that for?" she asked.

"The oil is an irritant. It'll give me those telltale red eyes that junkies tend to have." He slipped on a cheap pair of sunglasses. "Takes a few minutes to work."

"We got movement?"

"I think we're in luck." He handed her the binoculars.

She stared in the direction he indicated. "Either that or they're waiting for a ride to a Narcotics Anonymous meeting." She turned to him. "How do I look?"

They'd messed up the new clothes he'd bought, a sweatshirt and sneakers for her, and a flannel shirt for him by rubbing a jagged rock across the material, to tatter the fabric and scruff the shoes, giving their attire a worn-in appearance. If he'd had time, he would've gotten things from a thrift store to save them the trouble.

But her hair was pulled up in a smooth ponytail and her face too fresh and pretty to fit in.

"You need to be a bit rougher around the edges."

She removed the elastic band, fluffed her hair and redid the ponytail, making it sloppy with loose, chaotic strands framing her face. Pulling mascara from her purse, she flipped down the visor and lifted the cover of the vanity mirror. She applied mascara, but not to her lashes, and strategically smudged it underneath her eyes on the lids. She now looked like a party girl who'd had a hard night but was still beautiful.

"Much better."

They'd debated earlier and agreed it was best to play a couple. No way he'd be able to suppress his protective instincts if she was put in a compromising position.

"How much longer do you think until they get picked up?" she asked.

He shrugged. "No way to know for certain. Most of the

pharmacies around here open at nine, but Stryker said to be here early." He glanced at his watch. Seventy thirty. He popped open her glove box and shoved his primary burner phone linked to the voice-activated listening device at the clubhouse as well as his personal cell inside. "We should get out there. Try to blend in."

They exited her truck.

He braced against the frigid breeze with only an inexpensive fleece-lined windbreaker and the flannel shirt over his Henley to keep him warm. In a similar position, Ash shivered beside him as they crossed the street and turned the corner, heading toward the group.

They each had a backpack with protein bars, water, toothbrush, cheap burner phones that would be handed over in the event they were picked up and a rolled-up sleeping bag strapped to the bottom. Since he had no idea exactly what they were walking into, he erred on the side of caution.

With so many moving pieces, they didn't know where they would ultimately end up. So, he'd arranged for the same tow truck driver, Ganow, to collect her vehicle again and run it down to Laramie if necessary. Considering the exorbitant amount he was being paid, the guy didn't complain. Worst-case scenario, the drug dealers didn't show to pick up the group of addicts, there would be no need for the tow truck, but the guy still got paid. Win-win if you were Ganow.

As they neared the shelter, a scruffy guy with blotchy skin and an overgrown beard wearing a blue ballcap stared at them. The others noticed them but didn't take too much interest.

Once they were close enough, Rip gave a head nod to Mr. Bearded Blue Ballcap, BBB.

The guy didn't do likewise, only narrowing his eyes in

response. BBB was going to be a problem. The only question was how big of a problem.

Joining the seven individuals, they stood inside the shelter, shielded from the wind.

Rip put his back to a corner in the shelter, where he could see any approaching vehicles. Ash leaned her side against him, resting her head on his chest, and he curled a loose arm around her.

Six more strolled in while they waited.

An hour or so later, an unmarked white passenger van pulled up. The driver hopped out. A guy in his late twenties. Mirrored sunglasses. A well-worn leather jacket. Turtleneck. Torn jeans. Steel-toe boots. He finished smoking a cigarette and put it out under his bootheel.

He opened the passenger door and waved the group over.

Everyone filed out of the shelter and up to the van.

The man opened a drawstring bag and set it on the floor of the van. "You know the drill. Cell phones inside."

A guy stopped in front of the driver and extended his arms. The driver patted him down, probably checking for weapons and wires, and searched his knapsack. Then the guy dropped his phone in the bag and climbed into the van.

So on it went until it was their turn.

Rip stepped forward, with Ash behind him. He caught the flash of a gun in the shoulder holster beneath the man's jacket.

"Hold on, you weren't here last time."

"We couldn't make it," Rip said, gesturing to Ash.

The driver eyed him and then looked Ashley up and down, taking her in too closely. Rip chalked it up to male interest and not suspicion. Not that either was good. The latter meant trouble now. The former meant trouble later. No telling what those guys at the ranch expected from female junkies, who were normally willing to do anything to get their next fix.

Everything inside told him to persuade Ash to stay behind, but he was certain she wouldn't agree.

"I don't know either of you," the driver said.

With a sigh, Rip shook his head. "Well, LA does. I'm used to riding with her. This is my girl's first time. But LA will vouch for us."

The driver cocked his head to the side. "Oh yeah? You sure about that?"

Rip took off his sunglasses, squinting at the light. His eyes should be nice and red by now. "Positive."

The driver scrutinized him for a moment as if trying to decide what to do. "You willing to bet *both* your lives on it? Because if LA says she doesn't know you, I guarantee you'll each get a bullet in the head."

Hesitation would only convey doubt. Rip opened his bag and extended his arms for the pat-down as his answer.

The driver nodded. "Okay. I'm up for a game of Russian roulette. Let's see whether you live or die."

Rip was used to taking high-stakes chances as a Marine Raider, accomplishing the mission as his sole focus. What he wasn't willing to do was gamble with Ash's life. She was a competent and capable cop, but asking her to stay behind—when she'd refuse because she mistakenly thought being a cop meant she was cut out for this—would only raise a red flag.

They were in this now. He just had to make sure he kept her safe.

After a less than thorough pat-down, where the guy had missed the gun in Rip's ankle holster, he waited for his bag to be searched. In the few seconds it took, Rip noticed the tight weave of the fabric on the drawstring bag for the cell phones. Inside, it was lined with a shiny silver material. A Faraday bag—blocked GPS signals to prevent location tracking and stopped remote spying. Whoever this crew was they were serious players, but if they had weaknesses at the pickup point, there would be more later that he could exploit.

Rip dropped his burner phone in the bag, waited for Ash to be searched and to dump her burner as well. Then they climbed in.

The driver started the vehicle.

They rode for about ten minutes before pulling up in front of a shady-looking pain clinic on Elk Street. There were no other buildings on the block beside the shoddy one-story. The sign on the door read Closed.

"Come on." The driver cut the engine and ushered them out. At the exterior metal screen door, he rang the bell three times and waved at the camera positioned above it.

They were buzzed in, the lock disengaging. The driver held the door open. They funneled in, forming a line. One by one they were directed into an office that only had space for a small desk and chair. A man wearing a white lab coat, presumably the doctor, sat collecting IDs. Not bothering to raise his head and look at anyone or even speak, he entered information into a computer and then handed back the identification card along with twelve signed prescriptions per person.

The driver took a thick envelope from the inner pocket of his jacket, dropped it on the desk, and they left. In the van, he collected the prescriptions.

Next stop was a small pharmacy three minutes away. They parked right as the place opened for business. The driver handed each person a scrip, enough cash to pay for it, and herded them inside.

STANDING IN LINE at a higher-end drugstore in Fort Collins, Ashley shuffled forward. The pace had been grueling. A merry-go-round of stopping at pharmacies, everyone filing out with their belongings rather than leaving them in the van, turning in the prescriptions, little to no wait getting them filled—courtesy of working for drug dealers, they were paid in cash, and then off to the next location.

No big chain store pharmacies. Only smaller, independent ones, lots of mom-and-pop places. They spent around fifteen minutes inside, thirty at most, with the driver, whose name she'd learned was Drexel, always waiting outside out of view of the cameras. Most likely didn't want to be captured on the surveillance video.

Whatever agreement had been reached with the owners of the pharmacies had been done in advance.

Getting back in line behind her after using the restroom, Rip curled his left arm around the front of her, tugging her backpack against his chest, his fingers stroking her throat.

A wicked heat curled through her belly, pooling deep inside her, and the memory of last night flooded her mind. The way he'd held her. Caressed her. Tasted her. Gave her such intense pleasure. The only problem was it had all been one-sided. He told her how much he'd enjoyed it, making her writhe with want, hearing the sounds of her satisfaction, but it wasn't the same as them coming together as one.

He pressed his mouth to her ear. "You good?" Concern was heavy in his tone.

"Yeah," she said low. Her nerves had settled now that she understood this part of the process and knew what to expect. The next part, where they were off to the camp, would kick up fresh jitters.

Nothing she couldn't handle.

She was well trained. Not DEA agent or Special Forces

trained but ready, prepared for anything. She could get through this. Still, she was aware that Rip's protective instincts tended to kick into overdrive where she was concerned.

In front of her, the weird guy with the beard and ballcap stepped up to the pharmacist and handed over his prescription and ID.

"Not too late to back out," Rip whispered.

"As if." He needed to realize that her life wasn't more valuable than his. They could do this together, as a team.

"I figured as much. Just checking."

Her turn came. She followed the same procedure as the last eight times and then stepped to the side. Rip was the second to last to go up to the counter.

Those who had already turned in their prescriptions were already in the pickup line, paying with the cash Drexel had given them outside the store, and grabbing their white bag of pills.

"I'm going to go ahead of you," Rip said. "Use whatever time we've got to see if I can get Drexel to lower his guard a bit around me. If I can make inroads here, it'll be easier at the farm."

"Sure. I can buy you a minute or two by going to the bathroom. But I don't think it's going to be easy with Drexel."

He slid his arms around her shoulders, tugging her closer. "Speaking of not easy, things might get rough at the farm."

"I get it. I can do this." Security probably liked to have a good time with the women, trading sexual favors for pills, but she had Rip as an excuse. If she got cornered, a knee to the crotch would solve that problem. As for the countless other what-ifs, she'd take them one at a time.

He gave her a probing glance for a moment. "I know.

You wouldn't have gotten this far if you couldn't." His tone was warm, and from the look in his eyes, she could tell he meant more than this, here and now, but also the academy and every tough thing she'd been through as a deputy. "I believe in you." He gave her a quick kiss on the lips. "Do you trust me?"

She would trust him with her secrets, with her life. With her heart. "Of course."

"No matter what I might have to do, no matter what twists or turns come...*trust me.*"

"Always." But his words sent a jolt of nervousness rushing through her.

"Next!" the pharmacist called out, not bothering to use their names, seemingly anxious to give them their pills and get them—the dregs of society—out of their place of business.

Rip went up to the pickup counter, grabbed his white bag and headed for the exit.

Ashley turned to the woman with the humongous tote. "Go on ahead of me. I've got to use the bathroom." She started toward the restroom and glanced over her shoulder.

Rip was speaking to the security guard at the front door before he headed outside. He dropped his bag with the oxycodone into the larger bag that Drexel held open as he waited for them on the sidewalk.

Hurrying inside the bathroom, she took the opportunity to use the facilities and wash her hands. No telling how long until the next pharmacy or where. She left the restroom.

Only a couple of regular customers were in the store.

A tense-looking pharmacist waited for her. Ashley gave her the cash and took her bag with the oxy from the woman and headed down the aisle.

She was just about to reach the door and caught Rip's

eye. His attention flickered between her and Drexel. The two were engrossed in a lively conversation, with the driver appearing more at ease with Rip.

Perhaps it had worked.

"Excuse me, miss." The security guard stepped forward, blocking the door. "I need to search your backpack."

Her heart fluttered. "What? Why?"

"I have reason to believe you stole something."

"There must be some mistake."

"Please take off your backpack and unzip the front compartment."

Stunned, she slipped off the straps and turned the backpack around to face the security guard. "I didn't take anything."

"I hear that all the time from you people."

She didn't take the comment as racist since the guard was Black and attributed it to her being in a group of addicts.

Across the street, a police cruiser pulled into the gas station and parked. Two officers got out and went into the convenience store.

The security guard unzipped the front compartment of her bag and peered inside.

"Satisfied?" she asked.

Frowning, he pulled out two bottles of perfume. "This is three hundred bucks."

Ashley stiffened, her legs turning watery, not understanding how it got in her bag. "I didn't put that in there." Her mind spun trying to make sense of it.

"Sure, you didn't." The guard grabbed her wrist. "I've got to call the cops."

"What?" She tried to jerk her arm away without getting physical. The two officers stepped out of the gas station, holding cups of coffee, and lingered as they spoke. "No. We can talk about this."

"You can talk all you want to the police," the guard said.

Drexel shouted something at Rip and pointed for him to go over to the drugstore.

Rip yanked the front door open.

But it was Drexel who asked from farther back, "What's the problem?"

"She stole something. I've got to call the cops. It's a class two misdemeanor."

Ashley glanced at Rip to see how to play this.

His expression was inscrutable, his blue-gray eyes going stormy, and her chest constricted.

Rip looked over his shoulder at Drexel. "My girl's a hardcore junkie, sorry," he said to him. "She does stuff like this sometimes. She isn't worth this kind of trouble."

A cold chill splashed down her spine, numbing her heart. Ashley shook her head, not believing this was happening.

"We've got to go." Drexel turned, facing the gas station, where the officers still hadn't gotten back into their vehicle. "I don't need any headaches on this run. We cut her loose. Get her pills and we're out of here." The driver made a beeline for the van.

She was ready…prepared for anything. Except for Rip betraying her.

Her stomach felt as though it had dropped into the spin cycle of a washing machine, churning and flipping.

Why hadn't he pulled this stunt at the first pharmacy? Why now? Why wait all day until they got here?

All the way to Fort Collins.

They were in Fort Collins, where she had people that she knew, who could straighten things out and give her a ride. He'd been planning this the whole time.

Rip marched inside the store and snatched the white pharmacy bag from her fingers. She narrowed her eyes at him and gritted her teeth, too blindsided to speak, anger drumming in her veins.

"This isn't betrayal," he bit out, as if reading her mind. "It's protection. I won't play Russian roulette with your life. Call a friend and go home."

Then he turned his back and left her behind.

Chapter Twelve

The wounded look on Ash's face once she realized what he'd done had taken a slice out of his heart. Still haunted him. Those sultry brown eyes—that warmed him like a shot of whiskey when her heated gaze fell on him—had flared with shock and then narrowed to cold slits. But pain had washed over her expression.

Another pang wrenched through his chest. He didn't want her to think this reflected what he thought of her capabilities or was some sexist judgment on his part.

It was purely selfish.

If something happened to her, when he could've prevented it, he'd never forgive himself. Headed to the farm, he needed all his attention on only one thing. The mission. With no distractions.

Worrying about her rather than the task at hand would've split his focus and gotten them both killed.

Once they'd finished at the last pharmacy in Colorado Springs, they'd driven to a municipal airport east of the city and loaded onto a Cessna—based on the size he guessed a Caravan outfitted mainly for hauling cargo—where a grungy pilot had been waiting. They sat on benches rather than seats, and the aircraft took off.

The plane passed Devils Tower—a distinct, iconic butte

that loomed 867 feet above the trees—and began a descent to land. They were back in Wyoming. The far northeastern part of the state.

Rip stared at the roll-up door for loading cargo. It was the same kind used for skydiving.

The Cessna touched down on grassland with a bumpy landing and rolled to a stop.

Drexel got up and yanked on the wide door, getting it halfway before using both hands to finish rolling it up. "Come on. Everyone out." He hopped onto the ground and led the way to a parked van nearby.

Another man, who wore a skullcap beanie and glasses, was behind the wheel.

As they got off the plane, BBB elbowed Rip, shoving past him. He'd let it slide this one time. Causing a scene wasn't his goal, but he let that guy push him around and it would only end up being a bigger deal later.

Everyone climbed into the van and settled in for the ride. Ten minutes later they drove into a camp. Tents, makeshift shelters, a couple of decrepit school buses, and a fifth wheel camper and a large trailer both connected to trucks formed a horseshoe. This was the drug camp.

The van came to a stop, and they exited. Everyone began forming a line in front of a third guy, and he followed suit.

"Lumley, I'm going to see the boss," Drexel said to the current driver, holding up the bag from the day's haul.

Lumley nodded. Drexel headed for the fifth wheel camper.

The third guy was lean, rangy and not too tall, with scruff on his face. He stood handing out payment in pills. The line inched along steadily, everyone waiting their turn.

Rip scanned the area, searching for Lou-Ann. He wasn't

sure if she'd remember him. Plenty of bikers had crossed her path over the years.

Near a picnic table, he spotted her stirring a large pot of something situated over the fire. Her blond hair was in a choppy, angular bob. She'd put on some weight. No longer rail-thin, she had a little meat on her bones. He was tempted to head straight for her, but all the addicts were only interested in pills. So, he stayed in line to blend in.

BBB came up from behind him, elbowing him to the side, trying to cut the line in front of him. Rip was fed up with this guy and hooked BBB's leg with his foot, tripping him. BBB couldn't regain his balance. Momentum carried him forward and he face-planted into the dirt.

Not knowing when to back down, BBB jumped to his feet. "Who do you think you are?" he said, lunging for him.

Rip had his fist ready to punch the junkie in the face and ring his bell nicely.

But the one in charge of the line got between them. "No fighting. Or you're out of here." He turned to BBB and dumped one pill into his palm from a large container.

"Hey, where's the rest? I'm supposed to get three, Perry!"

"You fight, you get less. Next time keep the peace." Perry looked at Rip. "Same for you." He doled out one pill for him. "Go get something to eat." He gestured to the picnic table.

The others were in line in front of LA, getting bowls of soup and then grabbing things from the two cardboard boxes on the table. Rolls were in one and snacks in the other. People were walking away with protein bars and chips.

Rip increased his pace without trying to look overly eager. He couldn't have a real conversation with her while everyone else was hanging around nearby, but he at least wanted to give her a heads-up.

The door to the fifth wheel camper swung open.

Drexel hurried outside and ran to the firepit, where LA continued to serve soup. "Lumley," he called over the other one.

Another man appeared in the doorway of the camper. Curly hair. With his height and wide shoulders and the light creating a shadow behind him, he was a menacing figure. He lowered a respirator mask from his face and leaned against the jamb, watching.

That was no ordinary camper. They were doing something with drugs in there.

Rip approached the fire. His gaze met LA's and he held it, steady, confident.

Drexel pulled his gun and the addicts scattered like roaches, disappearing into the darkness.

Rip kept walking until the muzzle of the gun touched his chest.

"LA, do you know this dude?" Drexel asked. "He claims he was with you on some of your runs?"

Squinting, she stared at him and cocked her head to the side like she wasn't sure.

"We first met at Sturgis," Rip said quickly. "Benji—"

"Shut up!" Drexel moved the gun from his chest to his head. "She shouldn't need any reminders if she knows you."

Lumley drew a gun from his waistband at his back but kept it down at his side.

"Yeah, I know him." LA nodded. "Rip Lockwood. He's cool. My brother made the connect for him to do a couple of my runs."

With his name put out there, his exposure only grew. He couldn't catch a break. At this rate, he'd have to go deep underground for the rest of his life. Provided he survived the ranch.

Drexel lowered his weapon, put the safety on and returned it to his holster. "Your lucky day. You get to keep breathing. No hard feelings."

"None taken," Rip said.

Drexel and Lumley walked away.

The others kept a safe distance, giving Rip the opportunity he needed, but he didn't know how much time he'd have.

"What are you doing here?" LA asked in a whisper. "You're no druggie."

"So, you remember me."

She arched an eyebrow and looked him over from head to toe. "You're a hard man to forget, Rip. Explain. Why are you here?"

He grabbed a disposable bowl and went to the pot.

"I'd skip the soup if I were you." She glanced around. "They lace it with rat poison. They don't want the same druggies sticking around forever, giving the DEA a chance to turn one of them into a snitch. The steady regulars only last three to four months. Always plenty of addicts out there to take their place."

His stomach clenched. He set the bowl down. "Todd Burk is making a big play at home. Believe me, I want to see him hurt more than you do. I need to sever this pipeline of his, making him hemorrhage until he bleeds out." Rip grabbed a couple of protein bars from one of the boxes.

LA smirked, appearing downright devilish in the firelight. "Music to my ears. That SOB has it coming."

"I heard about your friend at Sturgis and what he did. I'm sorry. But she's just one in a long line of his victims." He thought about Angelo Russo. Todd's comeuppance was long overdue.

"Not sure how you're going to accomplish that goal."

"Maybe I'm a buyer, offer to pay for Todd's product at a higher price because of the war going on at home." Even if the DEA wasn't interested in the bust, some law official in the county would be. Setting up a sting was high risk, but also high reward.

"Won't work." LA shook her head. "Not unless you've got more than seven hundred fifty thousand dollars on you right now."

"What?" he said in a harsh whisper.

"Buyers pay up front in advance of receiving their product. Todd has already forked over seven fifty."

Where did he get that kind of cash? His operation must be much bigger than anyone thought.

"I've already put a bug in the boss's ear." LA zipped her fleece jacket and pulled on the hood. "Todd claims this is his last shipment from us. I've heard he intends to set up his own drug camp close to home. That he's already intimidating doctors and pharmacists. His plan will hurt our business. The boss isn't too happy about it. So, he's taking steps to make him pay. Pay big." She pivoted and nodded to the camper. "They've cut his entire shipment of product with fentanyl."

It wasn't uncommon for dealers to grind down pills, add fentanyl and use a pill press to reshape the drugs, making them resemble real prescription drugs such as oxy, Xanax, Adderall and much more. The process was time-consuming and tedious. The worst part was that dealers weren't chemists. It only took two salt-sized grains of fentanyl to be lethal. Dealers did it to increase profits, stretch their supply and expand the number of addicts by juicing the potency of the other drugs.

"The boss is being generous with the fentanyl in this shipment." She warmed her hands by the fire. "It'll probably kill a quarter of Todd's customers. The rest won't get the same high as his regular product and will go looking elsewhere. Namely us. Those who die will bring him a ton of heat from the authorities. This is going to be a lose-lose for Todd."

Not to mention the unsuspecting people, many of them college students, who'd be getting far more than they bargained for. So many kids were going to die to make Todd suffer.

Rip kept the horror from surfacing on his face. "You must be talking about a lot of fentanyl."

"We sell quite a bit. Get it from the cartel."

"Mendez?"

LA shook her head. "Sandoval."

"There has to be another way for me to get my hands on that shipment." He had brainstormed about other ways to accomplish the goal in the wee hours this morning and all day in the van. "When is it supposed to go out?"

She shrugged. "Not sure. Maybe Tuesday or Wednesday."

"Tell me about your boss?"

"Farley." LA glanced at the fifth wheel camper, and his gaze followed her line of sight. No one was outside besides Perry, who was smoking a cigarette near the travel trailer. "He's Canadian. Ex-military. The guys who fly the planes used to work with him."

That was his way in. "Can you introduce me? Tell him I'm interested in working as security for him. Making deliveries, runs, anything that pays well."

"Tricky," she said, raising her eyebrows. "The boss doesn't take a shine to everyone. Especially not strangers. I had to prove myself doing runs for a year before he moved me over to distro."

"How does the distribution work?"

"Varies. Local drops made from wherever the ranch is located at the time, we do by van. Farther out, we use one of the planes. Drop the load with a beacon. Buyer tracks it via GPS."

"I need to meet him."

"I don't know." Glancing around, she stuffed her hands in her pockets. "Get yourself situated in one of the buses. Claim a cot. I'll see what I can do."

"Hey, all I need is an intro. No need to vouch for me any further. I'll do the rest."

Chapter Thirteen

Ashley sat in the passenger's seat of the sedan. They'd passed the sign that read Welcome to Laramie, Home of Southeastern Wyoming University.

The college was the biggest draw to the town. She'd gotten her bachelor's degree in criminal justice while working as a deputy, considering it one more tool in her arsenal in the fight against Burk. When all along, her greatest tool was also her greatest weakness.

Rip Lockwood.

Her chest was tight, achy. Her heart swollen and bruised over Rip's deception. He wanted to sugarcoat his betrayal as protection, but it stung, nonetheless. Because it meant he didn't trust her enough to be honest.

She couldn't be mad at him. Not while he was out there risking his life to take down Todd Burk. If only he'd let her help, be his partner in this. She was the one who'd brought him in on the plan after all. Besides, this burden was both theirs to bear.

They passed the smaller, unassuming sign marking the border of Bison Ridge.

Ten minutes later, Jasper pulled up to her house and parked beside her truck.

Ashley donned her emotional armor and girded her feelings. "Thanks again. For the ride back to Wyoming. For coming down to the police station to clear everything up when Welliver wasn't available."

"It's really no problem." He flashed a kind smile. "If this is what it takes to get to see you again, then I don't mind. I wish you'd called sooner. But I still can't believe this Lockwood fellow. What was he thinking ditching you like that?"

One thing for her to question Rip, but Jasper wasn't allowed. "He was doing what he thought was right. To keep me safe."

"Doesn't he realize he isn't authorized to act on his own?"

Technically, neither was Ashley, but she didn't know how much Welliver had shared. "He's a Marine. Special Forces."

"Used to be a Marine. That was what, seven or eight years ago?"

Irritation flared inside her. "Once a Marine, always a Marine. Whatever the situation, he'll be able to handle it and when the time comes, he'll contact the proper authorities."

"Are you sure he's not going to go vigilante and ruin any chance of you building a case?"

If Rip were going to turn into a vigilante and take matters into his own hands, regardless of the law, Todd would already be dead and buried in an unmarked grave where no one would ever find his rotting corpse. "I'm sure. Thanks again." She clutched the handle and opened the door.

"Mind if I come in to use the bathroom?"

She tensed, but how could she refuse. He'd spent too much time at the police station straightening things out and then an hour on the road to bring her home. "Of course."

Hurrying up to the front door, she racked her brain on how to get rid of Jasper without being rude. This wasn't her forte. In fact, she'd never been the one doing the rejecting before.

She unlocked the door and let him inside. "The bathroom is right through there," she said, pointing down the hall.

Setting the backpack on the floor, she couldn't wait to wash her face, shower, and try to get some sleep. Though she doubted she'd be able to rest, not knowing what was happening to Rip.

The toilet flushed and the faucet ran in the two-piece bathroom. She had her spiel ready. It would be short and sweet and would hopefully work without ruffling any feathers.

A moment later, Jasper came toward her with a sweet smile.

Yawning like she was exhausted, she stretched. "Wow, it's so late."

"After that long drive, I'm parched. Can I have something to drink?"

Who would say no to water? Besides a rude ingrate. "Certainly." She led the way.

In her kitchen, she grabbed a glass from the cupboard and went to the sink, wishing she had bottled water that he could take to go.

"Now, this is the kind of drink I'm talking about," Jasper said, excitement in his voice.

She glanced over her shoulder as she filled the glass with water.

Jasper was holding her extravagant, decorative three-thousand-dollar bottle of tequila. "Clase Azul. Ashley, I had no idea you had such fine taste. The sheriff's department must be paying better than I thought."

"It was a gift. Birthday present from someone special." From someone who thought she was special.

"I've got to try a shot of this. It might be my only chance.

Do you mind?" Jasper beamed, his green eyes bright, his face warm, his blond hair perfectly coiffed.

He reminded her of the frat boys at SWU she'd hoped would ask her out and call her back for a second date, eons ago. It would've only resulted in what she'd found with Jasper.

Nothing of consequence.

She was done with boys who didn't excite her, who didn't know how to pleasure a woman in bed, whose loyalty ran surface-deep, who wouldn't put her above everything else.

Who were so consumed with taking that they didn't understand the true meaning of sacrifice.

"I do mind, actually." It wasn't about sharing. If the tequila hadn't been a gift from Rip, she would've gladly given the entire bottle to Jasper, regardless of the cost, simply to get rid of him. "If you drink, you'll use it as an excuse not to drive. I'd feel bad about asking you to leave and get behind the wheel with alcohol in your system. Then things would get awkward between us because I don't want you to stay."

His perfect smile fell. "But why? I don't understand. Did I do something wrong? I thought we were starting a good thing. Didn't you have fun last time?"

Sex was supposed to be fun and passionate and meaningful. With Jasper, she'd only checked the no-longer-a-virgin box. That was all.

What she'd shared with Rip had been in a different universe. Undoubtedly one-sided in her favor, he'd done things to her that she'd only read about, stopping short of letting him go to home base or letting her give him any of the sweet pleasure he'd spoon-fed her body, but she'd been as affectionate as he'd allow.

Connection—that was what she had with Rip.

Ashley dug out one of the plastic cups she used for her

protein shakes and transferred the water. "You're a nice guy, Jasper, truly you are. It's just… I'm seeing someone else."

Surprise flashed across his face. "So soon? Already? I didn't realize we were even over."

"We never really started." Two dinners, one night of humdrum sex, and no further communication. "Did we?"

"Welliver told me not to get my hopes up, but I was certain I had a shot at something more with you."

"Why would you think that when I haven't returned any of your calls?"

"I guess ghosting a person should send a clear message, but I kept coming up with explanations for it because it's never happened to me before."

Welcome to my world. "I'm sorry if I hurt your feelings. I should've had the decency to explain. I know better than most how it feels. You didn't deserve to be treated that way."

"No, it's okay," he said, giving her a crestfallen look. "Who's the lucky guy? Please don't tell me it's that old, washed-up Marine turned biker?"

"He's far from old or washed-up." *More like mature, high-skilled, could-probably-kill-you-with-a-pencil Marine.* "And yes, it is." No hesitation. No doubt. No shame. "I'm with Rip Lockwood."

What exactly that would mean in the days to come, she wasn't quite sure, but for now her heart wasn't interested in anyone else.

LYING ON TOP of his sleeping bag that he'd placed on a cot in the bus, Rip stared at the ceiling. His mind churned; his body was restless.

He hoped LA could work out the introduction that he needed. With close to a million dollars on the line, not to mention countless lives, if he could sabotage that shipment laced with fentanyl, it would be a deadly blow to Todd. A move like that would be knocking down the perfectly positioned domino and the rest would fall, an unstoppable chain reaction until Todd Burk was dead or in jail.

The floor of the bus creaked. Feet shuffling slowly toward him.

Rip spotted BBB trying to creep up on him. Sighing inwardly, he lowered his eyelids to appear asleep while watching this dude, who thought he was being stealthy.

BBB had something sharp in his hand, a knife or homemade shank. Whatever it was, it could kill him. Hunched low, BBB slunk closer, easing past his feet, up beyond his legs, and raised the weapon in his hand, poised to thrust it in his chest.

Rip swung his legs around, knocking the man to the side, and jumped up as he grabbed BBB. He wrenched BBB's wrist hard, enough to sprain but stopping short of breaking it, snatched the shiv from him and pressed the sharp tip of the weapon to his jugular.

"I'm the last guy in the world that you want to mess with," Rip ground out. "Come near me again and I'm going to flip your off switch. Got it?"

Eyes wide with terror, BBB nodded. "Y-y-yeah. Got it." He scurried away and scrambled off the bus.

LA passed the scaredy-cat on her way in.

Rip hid the improvised weapon in his pants.

"You're up," she said. "Farley will meet you, but you have one chance to make an impression. Don't blow it."

He took off his windbreaker and the flannel shirt he wore over the Henley. "I won't."

As he left the bus following LA, the cold air nipped him. A temporary discomfort he ignored. He spotted Perry carrying a batch of drugs from the camper to a shipping container that was eight feet by eight feet. He held parcels of pills in various colors, roughly the size of bricks, maybe sixty or seventy of them, bundled together in plastic wrap. It looked like a small bale of pharmaceuticals. Perry set it on the ground and unlocked the storage container.

The man with wild, curly hair waited in front of the travel trailer. To his left beside him, Lumley and Drexel were chatting and smoking cigarettes. In the golden lights under the awning of the trailer, Rip saw that Farley's hair was red, his eyes a watery blue, his face weathered with a long, jagged scar running across his left cheek.

Farley stood, peeling an apple with a switchblade, but Rip didn't miss the tactical knife holstered on his hip. It was a Karambit. The small knife had a razor-sharp double-edged blade that curved inwardly, nearly semicircular, ending in a vicious point. In action, with the large round steel finger holes on the handle, a Karambit reminded Rip of a tiger's claw. A nasty piece of business if the one wielding it knew how to use it properly.

The only other person Rip had encountered carrying one had been Special Operations like him.

"So, tell me, why should I give a junkie, who'll do anything for his next fix, two minutes of my time?" Farley asked.

Two was better than one. "For starters, I'm not a junkie."

Farley cast a furtive glance at LA, who started fidgeting.

Drexel pulled his weapon again and pointed it at Rip. The kid was too eager to draw. The skullcap-wearing Lumley wasn't sure what to do and grabbed his handgun as an afterthought.

Farley raised a palm, giving them the sign to hold, but Lumley was the only one to lower his weapon. "Let the man explain what he's doing here if not working for pills."

"My girl is a junkie," Rip said. "I'm here because I need serious work with serious pay."

"Oh, really." Farley slid a slice of apple into his mouth. "How do you feel about serious risk?"

"Wouldn't be here if I couldn't handle it?"

"Are you a cop?"

Tipping his head to the side, Rip pulled up his shirt-sleeves, revealing the tats that told his story from motor-cycle club to Marine Corps. "Do I look like a cop?"

Farley narrowed his eyes. "I don't like smart mouths."

With his 9mm still raised, Drexel took a step toward Rip.

"He's the Prez of the Iron Warriors," Lou-Ann said. "He ain't no cop."

Gritting his teeth, Rip wished she'd let him handle it from here.

"If you're the president of the Iron Warriors, why aren't you working with Todd Burk?" Farley asked. "Doesn't he have to kick back a part of his cut to the club?"

"We didn't see eye to eye on the percentage points. Long story short, Todd formed a new MC. The Hellhounds. Now, we're at war. I'm looking to stick it to him any way I can. Requires the right sort of friends and resources."

Farley stroked his jaw as he scrutinized Rip, especially his tattoos. "It's rare, but not unheard of for things to go wrong during deliveries. I happen to know that Burk is in-debted to the cartel. If he's not able to make a profit from his impending shipment, it would create trouble for him. The lethal kind. But I don't like blowback on my business."

"You mean, you don't like to get your hands dirty," Rip said.

The corner of Farley's mouth hitched up in a grin. "That's what middlemen are for. Let's say I hired you to handle Burk's next shipment. Free of charge to me, as a test. If his product happens to go missing, you take all the heat and deal with Todd Burk, so I never have to again. Dead men can't cause waves."

"What happens to the product?" Rip asked, though he already intended to turn it over to the DEA.

"Who's to say?" Farley shrugged. "If it got lost, finders keepers. But I'd want a taste of the profits."

"Ten percent."

"Forty. It's not as if you paid for it, and I remain your dealer in perpetuity."

Rip gave it a minute, pretending to weigh his options.

Clearly, Farley was a gambler. He was betting and betting big that Rip would eliminate Todd Burk for him, sell the tainted drugs, kicking back a whopping forty percent of the profits while taking the heat from the authorities once people started dying from the spiked drugs.

"You've got a deal." Rip offered his hand to shake on it.

Farley's half grin spread into a smile. "Not so fast. How do I know you're capable of *dealing* with Burk?"

Rip moved fast. He snapped his hand up, grabbing the body of Drexel's gun, and shoved the muzzle sideways to stay out of the line of any accidental discharge. Then he twisted the gun a half turn counterclockwise, nearly breaking Drexel's wrist. The gun fell to the ground. As Drexel howled in pain and clutched his wrist, Rip kicked the gun to the side into the darkness.

Keeping a lightning pace, he turned on Lumley. Skullcap was fumbling to draw his pistol. Once he pulled it free from his waistband, Rip snatched it. Stepping back, rather than aim it at anyone, he disassembled it. Removed the magazine. Ejected the bullet in the chamber. Pressed the two buttons on the side and slipped off the slide. Popped the spring free. Pushed out the barrel.

Eighteen seconds.

He held out the pieces for Lumley to take.

"A bit of a showoff, but I like you." Farley chuckled. "Were you MARSOC?" he asked, gesturing to Rip's tattoo of the Marine Special Operator insignia.

"Yeah. From the Karambit, I'd take it you were Canadian JTF," he said, using the acronym for the Joint Task Force.

"You'd guess correct." Farley's gaze dropped to his ankle. "You're also packing."

Rip tugged up the leg of his jeans, exposing the gun in his ankle holster. "What can I say? You've got shoddy security."

Drexel glared at him.

"Well, good help is expensive." Farley held out his palm and waited.

Reluctantly, Rip pulled out his gun and handed it over to him.

"SIG P365." Farley pulled back the slide, checking to see if a bullet was in the chamber. There was. "Nice weapon." He aimed it right between Rip's eyes. "I only do this kind of dirty business of backstabbing and double-dealing with people I can trust. Can I trust you, Rip Lockwood?"

No honor among thieves. Farley couldn't trust Rip any more than Rip could trust this drug dealer who had neglected to mention the entire shipment was laced with fentanyl.

"No. If I said yes, you'd know I was lying. What you can trust is that I'll take care of Todd Burk. He won't be your problem anymore."

Farley narrowed his eyes again. Then he cracked a smile. "As I said, I like you." He emptied Rip's magazine of bullets and handed it back empty. "Take a picture of Burk for me when you tell him his shipment got lost. I want to see the look on that weasel's face."

"I'll see what I can do."

This time they shook on it.

Chapter Fourteen

Dressed in civilian clothes, with her badge and her service weapon clipped on her belt, Ashley walked into the sheriff's department to let Clark know she was still breathing and to get an update on everything.

She kept her Stetson on, not intending to stay too long. Nodding hello to the deputy stationed at the front desk, she walked to the half door at the end of the counter and waited to be buzzed in.

The door clicked open. As she walked in, she glanced at the sheriff's office. He was inside talking to a striking, petite blonde.

Detective Hannah Delaney.

Her picture had been splashed all over the *Laramie Gazette* in recent months. She'd been put through the wringer. No law enforcement officer had gone through more hell than her, and Ashley did not envy the woman. However, Hannah had managed to catch the University Killer after nearly being his last victim, and gotten engaged to her partner on the case.

All is well that ends well. Ashley's grandmother used to say that.

Mitch flew out of his chair from behind his desk in the bullpen and hurried over to her.

"Where's the fire, Cody?" she asked, brightly.

Staring at her, he searched her face. "You haven't heard," he said in a whisper.

"Heard what?"

He took her by the arm, hauled her to the break room the size of a closet, stopped in front of the coffee maker and shut the door.

Drama was the last thing she needed this morning. "This is very cloak-and-dagger. What's up?" Then she caught the worry in Mitch's eyes.

"LPD released Todd Burk."

An icy wave of fear flooded every cell in her body. Fear for Rip. "No, no, they can't let him go." What if the Sons of Chaos reached out to him about everything that had happened in Happy Jack's? Not if. But when. Had they already called him? If so, would he think of contacting his supplier? Would he be able to? "I thought they were going to hold him for at least seventy-two hours."

"Detective Delaney had no choice but to cut him loose."

"But why? I don't understand."

With a sigh, Mitch put his hands on his hips. "The knife used to kill Shane Yates was the same murder weapon used to slit the throat of the pharmacist."

"Okay? What does that have to do with why they let him go?"

"We got prints off the knife. They didn't belong to Todd Burk."

"When have a set of prints at a crime scene ever matched his? It's probably some Hellhound who we need to interrogate because the odds are extremely high that Todd ordered the murder."

"You're not listening to me." Mitch clutched her shoulders as if to steady her, and dread crawled up her spine.

"We got a match on the prints. They belong to your biker boyfriend. Rip Lockwood."

Shock rocketed through her. What the hell?

She jerked free of his grip. "It's not Rip. He didn't kill anyone." Her mind whirled a second before focusing. "His place was burglarized Friday night. The knife must've been stolen."

Mitch looked anxiously uncomfortable. "You didn't list anything as missing."

"I meant to," she said quickly, without thinking. "It took him time to go through his things. He mentioned the knife was missing. But I didn't have a chance to report it because I had to go dark on something for the DEA." She grew lightheaded from the lie and the room started spinning. She hoped she didn't sound as suspicious as she thought she did.

Mitch frowned and crossed his arms. "What kind of knife was it?"

Swearing inside her head, she spun on her heel away from him. She pictured Rip. Sometimes he wore his Glock in a shoulder holster. Sometimes on his hip. She didn't know about the ankle holster. But he usually had a fixed blade. "KA-BAR." She opened the door.

Mitch slammed it closed. "Did he report it missing?"

"Let me open the door."

"If you march into the sheriff's office looking and sounding like you do right now, if you go in there and lie or try to protect Lockwood, you will lose your badge. Maybe not today, but when this all shakes out and the truth comes to light—"

"The facts, the evidence will prove without a shadow of doubt that Rip is innocent."

"Is he worth what you're about to do?"

"Yes." She tried to open the door again.

He leaned on it with his full weight, shutting it. "I'm your friend. Just walk back out the front door instead. Get in your car. Drive off. Calm down. Think it through. If what you're saying is true, then he doesn't need you to put up a defense for him in front of your boss. Let his lawyer do it for him."

"Move."

"Think it through, Russo."

"He didn't do this! If Rip was a cold-blooded killer, he would've taken care of Burk years ago."

"Right now, you need to be a deputy. Not his girlfriend."

Stepping away from the door, she took a deep breath. "You're right."

"I am?" Mitch cleared his throat. "I mean, of course I am. I just can't believe you're actually listening to me."

She needed to think clearly. Above all, she needed to be honest. Lying wouldn't help him.

"Did he really mention the knife was missing?"

She shook her head. "He hasn't had a chance to clean up his place, much less go through everything. But he wasn't wearing it when I was called over about gunshots reported. And I didn't see the knife on him the next day either. The three Hellhounds who broke in must have taken it from his trailer."

"Okay." Mitch nodded. "Just tell him to get a lawyer and turn himself in."

"I would…if I could."

"What is that supposed to mean?"

Her chest tightened with worry for Rip. "I need to update the sheriff on what I've been doing."

"And it concerns Lockwood?"

"It does." She'd dragged him into her one-woman operation to cut off Todd's drug supply and now he was alone, exposed. Vulnerable.

Because of her.

Lowering his head, Mitch sighed even louder this time. "Russo, what kind of hole have you dug for yourself?" Her friend looked at her with disappointment in his eyes.

"A big one." She held his gaze. "Please, get out of the way."

Mitch stepped aside.

She shuffled past him in the small space, opened the door and marched to the sheriff's office. Glancing across the hall, she looked at the empty chief deputy's office. She wished Holden Powell had been on duty today. Her brother, Angelo, had been Holden's best friend in high school. He'd have her back in this and would understand the lengths she had to go to in order to get Todd Burk. Knocking, she met her boss's gaze.

Sheriff Clark waved her in. "Deputy Russo. I'm happy to see you alive and well. This is Detective Hannah Delaney."

Ashley shook Delaney's hand while the detective remained seated. "Pleasure to meet you, ma'am. I admire your work and sympathize with everything you've been through this past year."

"Sometimes the job throws you into the meat grinder. If you're lucky, you come out in one piece, but never quite the same."

"I'm sure you've got some dark stories to tell."

The detective flashed a grim smile. "You have no idea."

"Detective Delaney, if that was all," Sheriff Clark said, standing, "I need to get an update from my deputy about a case she's working on."

"It would be best if she stayed." Ashley glanced between them as the sheriff's eyebrows pinched in curiosity. "What I have to tell you might have some bearing on her case."

"The Shane Yates murder?" Delaney asked.

"Yes."

"Well, go ahead." The sheriff gestured for her to speak.

For a split second, she debated how honest to be, but deep down she knew she had to tell him everything. "On Saturday, I left on a mission that was DEA-related."

"Yes." Clark nodded. "I'm aware."

Get on with it. Spit it out. "I misled you to believe that the DEA was sending me in with one of their agents. But they didn't feel the case warranted taking up their resources. They only want to go after big fish. Agent Welliver provided me with actionable intelligence, helped me strategize and then encouraged me to recruit Rip Lockwood as an asset and to have him assist me as my partner undercover, which is what I did."

Clark reared back, a stony expression washing over his features. His gaze flicked over her shoulder, behind her, to the hall. "Deputy Cody, unless you have a good reason to lurk outside my office, I suggest you return to your desk and get to work."

Ashley didn't bother to turn around; she could hear the shuffle of Mitch's footsteps hurrying off.

"Continue," Clark said, folding his arms across his chest.

Ashley clasped her wrist behind her back, standing formally at ease. "We went to Bitterroot Gulch on Saturday. Got information from the Sons of Chaos regarding Todd Burk's drug operation and then stayed the night in Misty Creek. I know that Shane Yates was killed that night between seven thirty and ten."

"How do you know that if you were out of town?" Detective Delaney asked.

"Because Bobby Quill from the Iron Warriors called Rip. I listened to the call on speakerphone. They all wanted to get information from Yates about the Hellhounds' drug operation. Yates responded to a text at seven thirty agreeing to meet them at their old clubhouse at nine. When he didn't show up, JD drove by his house. He saw the crime scene, you—" she nodded to the detective "—and a body bag. I also know that Rip's prints were found on the murder weapon."

The sheriff and Delaney exchanged a furtive glance.

"Explain," he said.

"I can't tell you how I know that, but I know for a fact that Rip didn't kill Shane Yates because he was with me that night. I can't speak to his whereabouts for the Fuller murder, but if the same weapon was used then it was the same person who committed both murders."

Clark glanced across at the bullpen through the window and shook his head, his gaze no doubt locked on Mitch. "What time did you leave town together on Saturday to go up to Bitterroot Gulch?" He opened his pad and grabbed a pen.

"We left separately, sir. But it's a three-and-a-half-hour drive to Bitterroot from here. He met me at Happy Jack's Roadhouse a few minutes after nine. We didn't stay long together inside. Maybe twenty minutes. We hung around the parking lot for another ten, waiting for Stryker, the president of the Sons. He gave us critical information that Rip is acting on now. Then we left and we were followed and shot at by three Sons."

"Can you prove Lockwood was with you in Bitterroot around nine last night?" Delaney asked.

"There were cameras outside of the roadhouse, which would have captured our arrival and departure." As well as their make-out session in the parking lot. "Also, I noticed a traffic camera at the main intersection less than a quarter mile on the only road that leads to Happy Jack's. We passed it separately on the way in and together on the way out. The motel we got a room at in Misty Creek also had surveillance cameras in the office. He was captured on it. I'm certain of it."

"Deputy Russo, did you and Lockwood share a room?" the detective asked.

Ashley stiffened. "The surveillance footage should be sufficient evidence to clear Lockwood of Shane Yates's murder. I don't see what bearing our accommodations would have on the case."

"You don't see, or you don't want to see?" Detective Delaney asked.

Ashley looked at the sheriff.

"Under normal circumstances," he said with a heavy breath, "I do my best to turn a blind eye to your association with Rip Lockwood because quite frankly I'd rather not acknowledge it. But since the nature of your relationship has significant bearing not only on a murder case but also a DEA-related operation, loosely related might I add and in a dangerous manner that I am not comfortable with, we need you to answer the question."

"We shared a room," Ashley admitted.

Detective Delaney crossed her legs. "Are the two of you involved?"

"It's complicated."

"I'll make it simple," the detective said. "Yes or no?"

"Yes. But as I've stated, there's proof that he was in Bitterroot at nine p.m. and could not be the person who murdered Yates. It is my belief that three Hellhounds broke into Rip's trailer on Friday to find something with his prints that they could use as a murder weapon. He injured one of them. A big, tall guy with a limp. Deputy Cody has the pictures I took of the three who I think are responsible for the break-in. Todd Burk is setting up Rip. I thought he wanted

172 Wyoming Undercover Escape

to kill him, but apparently framing him for murder is just as good to get him out of the way."

"To what end?" the sheriff asked.

"To have it all, with no opposition. Rip Lockwood is the one person that Todd Burk fears." Rightfully so because Rip had him in the crosshairs now. "The DEA-related operation was leading us to Burk's supplier at the ranch, a drug camp somewhere. But with Burk no longer being held in custody, Rip's life is in grave danger."

Detective Delaney straightened. "Wait a minute. Did you say a drug camp?"

"Yes."

"Before Yates was killed, he called me. Scared. Left a message that he had information about what Burk was planning next. Something about a *camp*, but it didn't make any sense at the time and I never got a chance to clarify."

"The drug camp that Stryker described was where they collected all the pills they received after a run. I rode undercover with Rip on part of one yesterday. They took us to a pain clinic. A doctor was paid to write various prescriptions for a bunch of addicts. For oxycodone, Percocet, Adderall. But mainly oxy. There was a man, Drexel, he was the driver and security, took us around to different pharmacies from Casper to Colorado Springs, though I only made it to Fort Collins, where we filled the prescriptions. Some kind of deal had been worked out in advance with the pharmacists. All smaller drugstores. Family-owned. Like Fuller's. Most just hurriedly went through the motions of filling the scrips to get us out of there, but a few looked as though they had been intimidated and coerced into compliance. What if Burk is trying to set up a similar operation here? And what if Mr. Fuller didn't want to cooperate and Burk found out that Yates was an informant, so he had them killed?"

Delaney was probably a fantastic poker player. Her expression didn't give away anything she was thinking.

"Ashley, it's not like you to color outside the lines," the sheriff said. "I want to know how long you've been misleading me about your work with the DEA, how deep it goes, and the specifics of everything you've done off-book. Anything you tell me will be fact-checked with Agent Welliver." Clark gave her a stern look of warning, but Ashley guessed that Welliver wouldn't return his calls until after he learned the results of the mission that Rip was still on. "Then I have to begin a formal investigation into your association, *relationship*, with Ripton Lockwood to see if it may have tainted any prior cases. Close the door and take a seat."

WEARING HER STETSON, Ashley walked out of the sheriff's office without her badge or service weapon. Suspended pending the results of the department's investigation.

White noise that had started in her ears as the sheriff began asking probing, invasive questions continued along with her out-of-body experience. It seemed she was floating to her truck rather than walking.

Sheriff Clark had doubted every word she said, she saw it in his eyes, but at least Detective Delaney had wasted no time starting the process to track down the surveillance footage in Bitterroot and Misty Creek. The Laramie Police Department would probably have it by lunch, certainly no later than the end of day, and Rip would be cleared of Shane Yates's murder and hopefully that of the pharmacist as well.

The only other good thing to come out of the interrogation was the three of them agreed Todd Burk was mostly likely behind this.

She climbed into her truck and simply sat there with no idea what to do next.

The loss of her badge didn't bother her. She only became a deputy for one reason and one reason only. To see Todd Burk behind bars. As long as justice was served, the results of the investigation didn't matter.

But she had no way to contact Rip and warn him that Todd was no longer being held in custody.

A buzzing sounded in her truck. She checked her cell phone to see if she had it on silent. But it wasn't coming from her cell.

The sound was coming from the glove box. She opened the compartment and tracked the buzzing to Rip's burner phone.

Ashley grabbed it. Instead of a phone number on the screen there was a six-digit code. She opened the flip phone and put it to her ear.

On the other end a bunch of men were cheering, whooping and hollering.

"All right, all right! Settle down. I told you I would be back lickety-split!" Todd Burk's voice.

Her pulse spiked. She stared at the phone, piecing together what she was hearing, how she was hearing it. Rip must have planted a listening device in the clubhouse.

She put the burner on speaker, took out her own phone and started recording.

"The cops can't hold me," Todd said. "No matter how hard they try."

"Teflon! Teflon! Teflon!" the Hellhounds cheered.

"Okay, let's get to business, boys," Todd said.

"Shane Yates is dead," a less than enthusiastic Hellhound said. "Murdered. You've got to call a vote for a member to meet Mr. Mayhem."

A vote to murder a brother in the club.

"Yates was a rat. He's been snitching." Todd went on to say foul things about Detective Delaney, calling her disgusting names. "He's not dead because of me. This is on her."

"We sided with you because you promised you'd be different." The same dissenter. "Rip didn't call a vote on you selling drugs, so we walked. On principle. But you're the same."

"I'm nothing like Lockwood!"

"You don't want to lead. You want to rule. That's not what we signed up for." Chairs scraped wood. She couldn't make out how many. Maybe three. Possibly four. "No member meets Mr. Mayhem without a vote. Snitch or not. We're out."

A door slammed.

"It's all right, boys. Let those weak punks walk. We don't need them anymore anyway. They served their purpose, sided with us in the vote that allowed us to form our own club. Now we can finish this with Rip. No vote necessary."

"He left town on Saturday," a different guy said. "Before Yates met Mr. Mayhem. He might have an alibi. Rip is one lucky dude. Maybe he can be persuaded to stay out of our way. He used to be our brother."

"Past tense," Todd said. "He's not a Hellhound. If he's not stopped, he'll bring down the empire we're building."

An empire of drugs and dirty money and death. Todd and his Hellhounds weren't building anything. Only destroying.

"Are you sure this is the best way to handle things?" a new voice questioned. "Letting Rip take the fall for the pharmacist and Shane? I mean, what if it doesn't work? Like Lyle said, he wasn't even in town when you had a brother killed. This might not stick to him and then he'll come for all of us. I don't know about you, but I don't want to be on his 'to-do things' list. Rip can be a scary, deadly dude when provoked. First you go after his deputy and now you frame him for murder. I'd call that provocation."

"Not me, *we*, brother. We're in this together," Todd said.

"I didn't vote for any of this!" a new dissenter called out. "I was in favor of expanding and starting our own drug camp. Not starting a war with Rip Lockwood."

"Quiet! Yeah, I wanted the cops to deal with Rip," Todd said. "So, I could see that self-righteous do-gooder rotting behind bars while I took everything that was his. Including his pretty deputy. But fortune shines on us, brothers. I heard from the Sons of Chaos. Guess who was in Happy Jack's with a cop the other night trying to get info on our drug supplier?"

"Rip wouldn't go in there with a cop, regardless of whether she's his old lady," someone called out.

"But he did! He called her his old lady, and they described her to me. Hot little number with light brown skin and long brown hair. Apparently, they were all over each other. We haven't seen Rip with a woman besides her. Definitely Deputy Russo. She must've lied to me the other day when I asked her about the two of them. Makes no difference now. I reached out to our supplier this morning. Just so happens Rip is with him. I told Farley that Rip is working with a cop. We don't have to worry about Lockwood anymore because his luck runs out today and I'm going to be there to watch. I've got the coordinates. Less than hour's drive north of town. All we have to do is go there and wait. He'll be delivered along with our drugs. Dead on arrival."

Chapter Fifteen

"Change of plans," LA said. "They upped the timeline for some reason. They're delivering Burk's shipment today. Be ready."

Change wasn't always good.

Rip finished eating the protein bar he'd purchased himself before arriving and washed it down with water. No need to take unnecessary chances consuming anything from the camp when all the food might be poisoned.

Putting on his windbreaker, he jammed the homemade shank into his pocket. He grabbed his backpack and got off the bus.

Perry went to the shipping container, unlocked it and opened the doors wide.

In the light of day, Rip had a full view of the contents. The quantity of drugs inside was staggering. A mother lode the DEA would salivate to get their hands on and be eager to take credit for the seizure of. This would make up for any wrongdoing on Ash's part or at least be taken into consideration if she were censured for breaking the rules.

Perry took a bundle of drugs out of the shipping container and locked it. The shipment had lashing straps crisscrossed and cinched tight around it. Hooked at the top was a small red device—the beacon.

"Load up!" Drexel called out.

The addicts crowded around the picnic table stopped eating and smoking. They gathered their belongings and began piling into the van.

Farley stepped out of the travel trailer, wearing sunglasses. His wild red hair was a hot mess in the wind. Taking a minute, he stretched his neck, arms, back, rolled his shoulders. Rip had done likewise before the sun was up. Farley slipped on a utility field jacket over his holstered gun and Karambit blade and started toward a second vehicle. "Rip!" He waved him over.

"Hey, what's up?" Rip asked, unease trickling through his veins.

"We're taking a separate plane to make the delivery," Farley said as Perry loaded the shipment into the van.

Rip stared at Farley. "You're coming?"

"I want to see to it that things go smoothly." Farley clasped his shoulder. "I need the warm fuzzy that you get to Laramie with the drugs. From there, it's up to you to deal with Burk."

Rip nodded, but his senses went on high alert. Farley preferred the middlemen to handle this sort of thing, so what was the real reason he was tagging along?

He suspected the answer meant trouble, but he played it cool. Got in the back of the van without protest or hesitation. Farley sat beside him.

Lumley drove with Perry riding in the passenger's seat.

A plane waited, engine running, on a landing strip that stretched off into vast, barren terrain punctuated by small piles of rocks. In the distance, trees, a range of mountains and Devils Tower were visible.

They parked and climbed out.

Lumley opened the back van door so Perry could grab

the shipment of drugs, but when he closed the door, he was holding a tire iron.

A blade or blunt instrument made the best weapon on an aircraft if you wanted to land in one piece. They boarded the plane without uttering a word. The aircraft was slightly smaller than the Cessna. A twin otter that had the same type of roll-up door.

Farley took a seat in the cockpit next to the pilot. With Lumley to his left, holding the tire iron, Perry to his right, Rip, on guard, buckled in.

The plane took off.

The two henchmen were antsy, gazes bouncing from the windows to the pilot, to Rip, to Farley.

None of this boded well for Rip. The lackeys didn't concern him. Farley was the unknown variable with his Special Operations background that made him wary.

They'd been in the air maybe forty-five minutes, definitely less than an hour, when Farley got up from his seat and shoved out of the cockpit. "We're here."

A shot of adrenaline that always came before a fight sparked through Rip's synapses. Muscles coiled. Ready for the inevitable moment to arrive.

Perry undid his lap belt. He went to the roll-up door, yanked it open, letting in a surge of cold air, activated the beacon on the shipment and tossed it out of the plane.

Hovering near the cockpit, Farley removed his sunglasses and slipped them into his top jacket pocket. "I got a call from Todd Burk this morning. He was released from police custody and couldn't wait to tell me that your supposed junkie of a girlfriend is a deputy with the sheriff's department. He also had a lot of colorful things to say about you. Like the only thing you'd do with a shipment of drugs is turn it over to the authorities."

"This is a war," Rip said, "and Todd's a liar. You can't trust anything he says."

"That may be true. In fact, it is true. Todd's a stinking liar for sure." Farley grinned, the facial expression tugging the skin around the gnarly scar on his cheek, making him look even more menacing. "But I'm going to take that weasel's word over yours on this because I know that he's a no-good criminal. Can't say the same about you." He pounded a fist on the wall of the cockpit. "Circle back around," he said to the pilot. Then he looked at Rip. "Time to jump."

"No parachute?" Rip asked with a wry smile.

Farley chuckled. "Why couldn't you be on my side of the law? I wasn't lying when I said I liked you."

"Get up." Lumley nudged Rip's arm. "And get moving. Burk is down there waiting to see you hit the ground. We promised him a show."

"Well, we don't want to disappoint him," Rip said, but it wasn't going to be him hitting the ground like a pancake if he had anything to say about it.

Lumley shoved him this time. "Let's go."

Near the open door, Perry stood hunched from the low ceiling, waiting for him.

Rip shook his head. "No way."

Staying back near the cockpit, Farley simply watched.

Lumley moved the tire iron to his left hand and grabbed the hilt of the 9mm stuffed in the front of his waistband with his right. "Unbuckle your belt. Now!"

Rip was seated at such a close range. The odds were high that Lumley could get off a shot and hit him somewhere that would do plenty of damage without puncturing a hole in the aircraft.

So, Rip did the only thing he could. He unbuckled his lap belt and got up.

Then Perry made the mistake of moving forward to grab him.

Training kicked in. Rip was a machine, programmed by the Marines for one purpose: to put down the enemy.

He fired a left-handed jab to the man's solar plexus, a tight network of nerves below the sternum, knocking the wind from him as he doubled over. Not giving Perry a chance to regain his breath, Rip grabbed him and whirled 180 degrees in anticipation of Lumley's next move.

Sure enough, in a panic the jerk had already pulled his gun. Lumley squeezed off two rounds. One bullet struck Perry in the back and the second in the head.

"Don't fire, you fool," Farley shouted. "You'll get us all killed."

Dropping the dead guy, Rip backed up closer to the door and prepared to take down the next one.

With a deer-in-the-headlights look, Lumley lunged at him. The guy swung wildly with the tire iron, but Rip pivoted out of the way, and Lumley hit nothing but air.

Rip launched a punch to his windpipe. When Lumley dropped the tire iron and gun and clutched his throat with both hands, his mouth open, struggling to breathe, not even a wheeze getting out, Rip knew he'd crushed his windpipe. He thrust Lumley toward the open door and kicked him out.

Something hard came down across Rip's skull, and piercing pain tore through the side of his head. The world blurred. He dropped, his head slamming against the steel bench, and hit the floor.

Farley. Farley had hit him with the tire iron. The former JTF operator had moved quick as lightning because he was also trained to kill.

Rip tried to regain his bearings, tried to swim through the dizzying haze of pain.

Move. You have to move.

Every second counted. He needed to end this fight quickly or the other guy would.

Farley yanked his leg, hauling him to the opening.

Frigid air rushed over Rip, energizing him. Adrenaline fired hot in his system, clearing his mind, but his head throbbed like someone was beating on his skull with a chisel.

Grabbing him by the windbreaker, Farley managed to shove Rip's head and shoulders out the door.

But with his right hand, Rip snatched onto a strap dangling near the rear wall, used for tying down cargo, and held strong.

Rather than trying to wrestle him out of the plane as one of his lackeys might've attempted, Farley drew his Karambit knife, hoisted the blade up and drove it down.

Rip reacted without hesitation, without emotion, without thought, and blocked with his left hand.

The blade plunged into his palm. Ignoring the excruciating pain, disregarding the fear of falling out the aircraft and plummeting to the ground, Rip let go of the strap keeping him onboard and grabbed the shiv from his pocket. Then he thrust the pointed end of the improvised blade up under Farley's chin.

The redheaded man stilled, a shocked expression on his pale face. Rip pulled the weapon free and stabbed again. This time in the jugular. It was done. Blood ran down Farley's throat, dripping onto Rip. He shoved Farley off him, knocking him deeper into the plane, and the former JTF operator keeled over.

Scrambling away from the door, Rip yanked the knife from his hand, letting it clatter to the floor. Not taking any chances, he checked Farley. The man was dead, his eyes open and vacant.

Rip peered out the door. Below on the ground, he spotted a black van and a couple of motorcycles—Hellhounds—in a wide-open space. The Snowy Mountain Range wasn't far to the southwest. They were somewhere north of Laramie, with no town around for miles.

Just then he caught sight of patrol cruisers from two different counties racing up, red-and-blue lights flashing. They surrounded the Hellhounds from the west and south, cutting off any escape.

Rip caught his breath, grabbed a gun and shuffled to the cockpit. Keeping the safety on, he aimed the weapon at the pilot.

"Don't kill me," the middle-aged man said, his eyes growing wide.

"I'm not going to kill you. But you are going to land. Right down there."

The pilot looked around at the ground. "I don't think there's enough room to taxi before I can stop."

"You had less space where you picked us up. Do it."

"Uh-uh." The pilot took another glance. "Pretty rocky down there. We could crash."

"I said I wouldn't kill you, but it's about to get a whole lot rockier for you if I shoot you," he said, aiming at the man's knee. Not that Rip needed to go that far. The pilot was scared of the cops. Rip needed to override that fear with the prospect of something worse. "Take us down and land."

After a moment longer of hesitation, the pilot nodded. "All right."

Rip's head pounded and ached. "You got a med kit?"

The pilot gestured to the wall behind the seat.

Rip popped open the kit, dug out some gauze and medical tape.

As the pilot circled twice, gauging where to make his approach, Rip quickly bandaged his hand, though it wouldn't do much to stop the bleeding. Once the pilot finally decided, he brought the twin otter down, taxied and braked to a stop.

"You're getting out first." Rip waved him along with the gun, and the pilot moved to the back of the plane.

The blood from the wound in his palm had already soaked through the gauze. Getting up, Rip winced from another gut-wrenching stab that went through his head, his vision blurring again. Pure adrenaline still pumping through him was muting the pain and keeping him moving. But it wouldn't last. He dreaded to think what state he'd be in once it wore off.

The pilot hopped out onto the ground and raised his palms.

Rip dropped the gun before he eased off the plane and held up his hands.

Several Hellhounds were in handcuffs. Freddy, Arlo and Clive—the same ones he suspected had attacked him at his trailer. They were loaded into the backs of cruisers.

And Todd Burk. He was down on the ground, face-first, arms behind him, a knee in his back, as he was being cuffed. As they hauled him up, his gaze found Rip's.

Seething, Todd glared at him, and Rip smiled even though it cost him a jolt of pain.

Deputies from the neighboring county approached him and the pilot, guns at the ready, issuing instructions.

Doing as told, Rip and the pilot got down on their knees and put their hands behind their heads.

A door from one of the Laramie cruisers flew open. Ash

jumped out and ran, headed straight for him. She shoved past Sheriff Clark, who tried to hold her back, and kept sprinting for him.

Rip's heart lit up brighter than a stadium on Super Bowl Sunday.

Sheriff Clark hurried behind her. "It's all right!" He shouted to the other deputies. "Let her through. Rip Lockwood is with us."

For a split second, Rip wondered why she'd been inside the vehicle in the first place and why the other deputies didn't already know she was with the sheriff's department.

But every thought evaporated once she was in front of him, helping him up from the ground, her face slack with shock, her eyes wide with worry.

"Oh my God!" Ash's gaze fell over him. "You're covered in blood."

"Most of it is not mine." Grateful to be alive, he wanted to hold her, kiss her, but he was a bloody mess and there wasn't much time. His vision blurred again. Pain ballooned in his head like his skull wanted to explode.

Sheriff Clark came up beside them. "Good grief. What happened to you?" He glanced inside the plane and gasped. "Or rather, I guess you're what happened to them."

Ash touched the side of his head, and he winced. "You're bleeding. We need to get you to the hospital."

A deputy slapped handcuffs on the pilot.

"You're going to need him," Rip said, gesturing to the middle-aged man, "to fly you back near Devils Tower, where he picked us up. From there, it's a ten-minute ride…" He pushed through the fog encroaching on his brain to think. "Due east. You'll find the drug camp. Agent Welliver will want to know. There's fentanyl from the Sandoval cartel and enough drugs to make it more than worth his time."

He kept spewing every little thing he could remember. "Farley was in charge, but he's dead in the plane. Lou-Ann, LA, she knows about the dealings with the cartel and Burk. If someone cuts her a deal, she'll talk." He thought about her serving rat poison to the addicts they used as workers. "But the deal shouldn't be too good."

"Okay." Sheriff Clark nodded. "We'll take care of it."

"Come on." Ash curled an arm around his waist, slinging his left arm over her shoulder, like he needed her help walking.

And maybe he did, because a blinding bolt of pain lanced his head.

He took four steps forward, the world spun, and everything faded to black as his legs buckled.

Chapter Sixteen

Numb. Ashley was numb as she continued to wait for Rip to open his eyes and talk to her. In his hospital room, she lay in the bed alongside Rip, her head on his shoulder, her hand on his chest, listening, feeling him breathe on his own. The blinds were drawn, dampening the afternoon light without making the room too dim.

The hardest part had been the thirty-six hours he was in the ICU on a ventilator. The nerve-racking sounds of the machine, the overwhelming smell of disinfectant, constant reminders of how close he'd come to death. She didn't know if she could bear any of this, how to face the prospect of him not making a full recovery. So, she'd pushed such thoughts from her mind. As she'd sat in the chair, holding his hand and watching over him, one thing repeated over and over in her head.

I can't lose you.

I can't lose you.

Once he was moved to a regular room, relief had set in, but she still couldn't bear to leave his side for more than a few minutes. Not until he woke up. He was only here in the hospital because she'd dragged him into all this.

Ashley was considering going to the cafeteria for a cup of coffee when Rip stirred and finally opened his eyes.

Leaning up on her forearm, she peered down at him.

His gaze wandered before landing on her. "Hey, you." He sounded foggy.

She caressed his cheek, so happy to see him awake tears pricked her eyes. "Hey, you."

"My throat…"

"You were intubated," she said, and his eyes narrowed in confusion. "Want some water?"

He nodded. Groaned. Struggled to sit up.

"Take it easy." She helped him adjust and then grabbed the cup that she had ready for him. Once he was propped up and seemed more comfortable, she put the straw to his lips.

Rip sipped generously, draining the cup of water. "How long was I out?"

"Two days."

"Two?" He was quiet for a long moment. "Have you been here the whole time?"

"I have. I didn't want to leave you." She got an extra pillow from a table near the chair, put it behind his head and climbed back into the bed. "They put you into a medically induced coma to alleviate the swelling in your head and allow your brain to rest. You opened your eyes after they took you off the ventilator, but you fell back asleep. The doctor said it was from the medication, but that you're a remarkable healer." She rubbed his arm. "You're going to be fine."

He raised his left hand that was bandaged and clenched his fingers until he winced.

"Nineteen stitches," she said. "You're very lucky according to the surgeon who operated on your hand. Well, that's what everyone around here is saying. All the doctors and nurses." She caressed his cheek. "Which makes me lucky."

He lowered his eyes. "Are you still angry that I left you behind?"

"No." Her worry and fear for his life overrode any anger. "I understand why you left me in Fort Collins." If he was in better shape, she would've told him who had given her a ride home, but in his current condition she didn't want to risk upsetting him.

"What happened with the camp?" he asked.

"A major drug seizure for the sheriff's department and DEA. LA was arrested. She was willing to spill her guts about everything for a lighter sentence. All thanks to you."

Reaching for her, he brushed strands of hair from her face. "Thanks to us. That bust never would've happened if not for you. Your stubborn persistence. You're the one who got the lead from the DEA and made sure I didn't waste time getting up to Happy Jack's. If I had waited a day or two, planning, trying to handle it on my own, we would've missed the window of opportunity and Todd would've gotten his last shipment. Did Agent Welliver cover for you with Sheriff Clark?"

"He did. Spoke very highly of me and commended my efforts in recruiting you." But she had already been honest with her boss and nothing Welliver had to say was going to undo her suspension or could help with the internal investigation.

"Is everything okay with your job?" he asked, as if reading her mind.

The man had nearly died, and he was worried about her. "It's complicated. We can talk about it later. I'm just happy you're going to be okay and that Todd Burk is finally going to prison for a long time."

"They did catch him red-handed picking up a shipment of drugs."

"And we have a recording of him admitting to framing you for murder."

"Murder? What did I miss?"

"A lot. Is your KA-BAR knife missing?"

He thought for a moment and then nodded. "Yeah. I left it in my trailer. Those guys broke in and I couldn't find it afterward."

"They stole it. Used it in the murders of Dr. Fuller, the pharmacist, and Shane Yates. But I was your alibi for Yates. There's surveillance video of you in Bitterroot, proving you couldn't have been here in town at the time of his murder."

"How did you get the recording?"

"The burner phone you put in my glove box rang."

"The bug I planted in the chapel, the meeting room, must have been voice-activated. I forgot to tell you about it."

"When I answered the phone, I heard Burk bragging about everything. Including how his supplier, Farley, was going to kill you that day. I recorded it on my phone, but I was out of my mind with worry for you." With fear like she'd never known. She held his face in her hands and kissed him lightly.

But he moved his mouth from hers, and unease wormed through her. "The Sons of Chaos will be coming for me sooner or later. Word will get out about LA to the Sandoval cartel and then I'll be on their radar, too. I'm leaving town, Ash. Today."

She swallowed around the sudden lump in her throat. "You're not going anywhere today. They're running some more tests on you later this afternoon and the doctor needs to determine if you need rehab."

"I can do rehab anywhere. *If* I need it."

"The doctor isn't going to discharge you today."

"This isn't prison. They can't keep me against my will. I'll leave when I'm ready regardless of paperwork."

Putting her hand on his chest, she held his gaze and softened her voice. "You had a severe head injury. Let them finish running their tests today, to make sure that you're fine. It takes hours to get results." Everything in the hospital took forever. One long waiting game. "Tomorrow, if you're still determined to get out of here, you can do it then. Please. For me. For my peace of mind."

He sighed. "I'll wait until tomorrow," he said, and she smiled. "Only if you agree not to stay."

Her smile fell. "What?" Drawing closer, she rested on her elbow, lowered her face close to his and cupped his cheek. "Don't do this. Don't push me away. Not after everything we've been through together."

"You've been in this hospital for two days. Get some air. Go rest. Do something else besides fret over me. I'm fine."

"You're *going to be* fine. Provided you take the time to heal and listen to the doctor. You're not invincible."

"Never thought I'd see the day where you were begging to keep me in bed."

His flirty banter was back, which meant he was truly on the road to recovery.

"You could have plenty more of those days." She brushed her lips over his and held his gaze. "You just have to want them. Want me."

Someone near the door cleared their throat, drawing their attention.

Quill and JD entered the room.

"Sorry to interrupt," Quill said. "We can come back later."

"No." Rip waved them in. "Ash was just leaving."

"To get a cup of coffee," she quickly added and glared at him. "I'll be back." Then she leaned in, bringing her mouth to his ear. "Whether you like it or not. If you think you're going to slip out of the hospital and sneak out of town, think again." Putting her hand on his chest, she snuggled up close and kissed him on the lips in front of his MC brothers. The long, slow kiss left no doubt about her feelings for him, and maybe because they had an audience or he was too tired to fight her, whatever the reason, he kissed her back, soothing her heart.

She climbed out of the bed, grabbed her purse and, ignoring the confused stares of the Iron Warriors, left the room. In the hall out of sight, she stood still a moment and listened.

"You're welcome, brother," Quill said with an attitude.

"What are you talking about?" Rip asked. "Welcome for what?"

"For her. Looks like she's your old lady after all. And that would not have happened if we hadn't been scaring off every dude that came near her."

"I'm still not happy about your interference, but I don't know what she is," Rip said. "What I do know is that I have to leave town as soon as possible and she's not coming with me."

We'll see about that, Ripton Lockwood.

Rip was a man of his word. The measures he'd taken over the years had derailed Ash's love life. Now that Todd Burk was in jail on charges that were going to stick, she could be free. To live her life as she wanted. To date. To have fun. To find love. To settle down in town, where she had a career and her family and roots.

Not running away and going into hiding with him.

"Have you heard anything from the Sons?" Rip asked.

JD nodded. "Oh, yeah. Stryker found out his sister is in jail because of you. The Sons want your head on a pike."

"Your old lady's, too." Quill raised his eyebrows.

"They asked the Hellhounds to take care of you two,"

JD said, "but they're a mess after Todd and the others got busted. At least that's what Will tells me."

Will was one of the surprise voters that had been against Rip because he hadn't trusted in the process and in the members to make the right decision.

Rip believed that deep down, Will was still loyal to the Iron Warriors and under new leadership, he'd return.

"Get the word out that Ash is with the sheriff's department. It'll be a deterrent. Once the Sons know I'm gone and I've left her behind, they'll think I don't care about her. But before I leave, I'll talk to Sheriff Clark about getting her protection and give him enough information to take to the FBI about the Sons and their prostitution ring. That'll put many of them in jail and leave the rest in real chaos." LA didn't know about Ash, which meant she'd stay under the radar of the cartel.

JD crossed his arms. "You can't go starting a war with the Sons by giving the FBI information without a vote, Rip."

"You heard Will. They want me dead. I'm already at war with them. That's why you need to strip me of my patches and excommunicate me. To protect the Warriors from any blowback."

Quill blanched. "No. No way. We won't do it. There has to be another alternative."

"There isn't." Rip had given it serious consideration. Strategized all the options. "Quill, I want you to support JD for president."

JD shook his head. "I don't want the mantle."

Smiling, Rip understood what the others had tried to teach him years ago. "That's one of the reasons why you're perfect for the job. You'll do great."

Ashley walked back into the room, holding a cup of coffee. She stopped at the foot of his bed and met Rip's gaze, and his chest tightened. She was so beautiful. So full of light. Special.

He didn't want to leave her, but he also didn't want to endanger her.

The best thing to do was to set her free.

"I appreciate everything you guys have done for me," Rip said to them. "Everything I've asked. For trusting me. For having my back. For watching out for Ash." He took a breath, finding it difficult to continue. He wasn't the sentimental type but was getting a bit choked up. "Even though I won't be an Iron Warrior anymore, you'll always be my brothers."

Ash stiffened, her eyes going wide in surprise.

"One drink before you leave town?" Quill asked.

Rip gave a noncommittal gesture. "I can't make any promises."

"I don't want this to be the last time I see you. In a hospital bed. Not wearing any underwear." Quill grinned.

Rip chuckled. "I'll see what I can do."

"You were a great Prez, Rip. I learned a lot from you," JD said.

"Make me proud. Lead them in the right direction."

Quill and JD took turns tapping a fist on Rip's shoulder. On their way out, they did the same to Ash.

There was a knock on the door. Chief Deputy Holden Powell came in and tipped his cowboy hat in greeting. He was the one man Rip thought might've ended up with Ashley. He had been her brother's best friend. Holden and Ashley had chosen to be deputies at the sheriff's office, and worked long hours together. But according to Ash, Holden always treated her like a little sister and now was happily married to a nurse.

"Holden," Ash said, "what are you doing here?"

"I wish it was better news," the chief deputy said gravely.

JD eased toward the door. "We'll get going."

"You two might want to hold on." Powell stepped deeper inside the room. "Since it's Thanksgiving tomorrow, the district attorney wanted Burk and the other three Hellhounds to be moved to county lockup today. Earlier, as they were being transported, they managed to break out."

Rip swore under his breath. *Teflon.*

"In the process, they killed Deputy Livingston and injured Deputy Cody," Powell continued.

"Oh no!" Ash moved closer to Powell. "Is Mitch going to be okay?"

"He's out of surgery. Lost a lot of blood. Needed a transfusion. But he's going to make it."

Ash's face hardened. "You should've told me sooner."

"I'm sorry. I know you two are good friends, but you were waiting for Rip to wake up. I didn't want to add more to your plate of worries until I had to. The US Marshals have started a countywide manhunt for Burk and the others. In the meantime, we're working with the Laramie Police Department to have an officer assigned to each of you around the clock," he said to Ash and Rip.

Todd and the others would be looking for a place to hide. Someone vulnerable, someone alone whom they could exploit. "Ida. She'll need protection while I'm in here."

Holden tipped the brim of his hat up. "The LPD can only spare enough personnel to watch each of you."

"Ida is fine." Ash came around to the side of the bed and put a hand on his arm. "She's been with my parents the last few days."

"She went willingly?"

Smiling, Ash nodded. "Not a single complaint."

Didn't sound like his Aunt Ida.

"My mom had been checking on her several times a day to make sure she was all right and was taking her medication. Eventually, she just invited her to stay over. Ida seemed more than happy to have the company," she said, and that was a great relief to Rip. Ash turned to Powell. "You can have one officer watch our family. The other one can cover both of us. We'll stay together."

She was good at boxing him in and getting what she wanted. He'd give her that.

But *our family* struck him in an unexpected way. It almost gave him hope he and Ash could be together, their families joined as one.

Powell looked at Quill and JD. "We're hoping the Iron Warriors could keep an ear out and let us know if you hear anything."

JD nodded. "Of course. The sooner you catch them, the better for all of us."

"Everyone needs to stay vigilant," Chief Deputy Powell said. "Todd Burk and his cohorts are armed and desperate. With the marshals searching for them, we think it won't take long for them to be apprehended."

Ash's gaze found Rip's. The look in her eyes made his heart constrict. Too many emotions surfacing, battling for dominance. He didn't like it clouding his judgment, thawing him when he needed to be ice-cold—the only way to make tough decisions.

"I'm still getting out of the hospital tomorrow," he said to her. "But I won't leave town. Not until Burk has been captured."

Chapter Seventeen

In her parents' kitchen, Ashley finished putting away the last of the food. "I really appreciate you going to so much trouble to make Thanksgiving special."

"It was nice to have more people at the table this year," Mom said. "Instead of it being the three of us. And I'm pleased you finally brought a man to dinner. I didn't expect it to be that one, a biker, but you seem happy around him. Light up whenever you two are in the same room. Your father and I have noticed how he looks at you, too."

"How is that?" She still wasn't sure what was going through Rip's head.

He acted determined to push her away, but she was known for her stubborn persistence.

Mom gave a knowing smile and a soft chuckle. "The man is in love with you."

Air caught in her throat. *In love.* Their relationship had been a complicated, slow burn and then a sudden rolling boil. He'd give his life for her, and she wanted to spend her life with him. Love…was the perfect word.

"Are you sure?"

"I'm certain of it. The real question is how do you feel?"

She went to her mother and took her warm hands in hers. "I didn't realize how deeply I felt for him until I saw him covered in blood and watched him collapse. Sitting with him in the hospital, I would've given anything for him to open his eyes. Anything."

"I never knew what to make of Rip, but after everything he went through to get Todd Burk arrested, he's got our approval. We just want you to be happy."

"I will be. Once Burk is back behind bars." And Rip accepted they were meant for each other. "Tomorrow, I need to sit down with you and Dad and share my plans for the future."

"Not tonight?"

Ashley needed to get Rip on board with the plan first. "Tomorrow." She hugged her mom. "I love you."

"I love you, too, sweetheart."

She went into the living room.

Rip and her dad were coming down the hallway from the bedroom.

"We just tucked Ida in for the night," Dad said.

"She really loves it here. Thank you for taking care of her while I was gone." Rip shook her dad's hand. "There's something I'd like to ask, though it might be a huge imposition."

Ashley sensed what it would be. "Rip, I think you should wait until tomorrow. We'll come back. Okay?" One clear discussion about leaving would be best. "It's late and I'd like to get going."

Eyeing her, Rip hesitated.

She looked away from him and hugged her dad. "See you tomorrow. Love you."

"Love you more, jelly bean."

Hating when her dad called her that, she groaned.

Rip followed her through the living room.

She opened the front door and stepped out onto the porch. "An officer will stay parked out front until the US Marshals find Burk and his crew."

"Don't worry about us. You two go enjoy the rest of your evening." Dad lingered in the doorway, watching them get into her truck, and waved as they drove off.

"Drop me at my trailer. The other officer will stay with you."

"Rip—"

"Ash, we're not going to argue about this. I said I won't leave town. I'm not going to run off."

"Fine, no arguing." She turned on the radio and drove. Ten minutes into the ride, rather than take the road that led to the Hindley property, she took a left, heading for Bison Ridge.

"This isn't the way to my place."

"No, it isn't, because we're going to mine."

"Ashley."

"Is that going to be a thing?"

"Is what?"

"You using my whole name when you're cross with me?"

"I want to go to my trailer."

"The one you haven't cleaned up? Sure thing. But first, I want to show you something."

"Okay. I'll play this game. What?"

"Something you've never seen before."

He growled, the low rumble in his chest sounding sexy instead of scary. "Tell me what it is."

She pulled up in front of her house and threw the truck in Park. "That would spoil the surprise. But trust me, it's important. Afterward, I can take you straight home, if you still want to go," she said, and he narrowed his eyes at her. "I'd take that deal if I were you. It's the best one you're going to get." She pocketed her car keys.

"Fine." He got out, slamming the truck door, and stomped up to the porch.

The police officer parked behind her vehicle.

She went to the driver's side of the patrol car and he rolled down the window. "We're going to be here for the rest of the night. Can I get you some coffee or something?"

He held up a thermos and a plate of dessert covered in plastic wrap. "Your mother was kind enough to take care of me and the other officer who is watching your family's house. Have a good night."

"Thank you." It was a shame those officers had to be out in the cold, keeping guard on Thanksgiving, but hopefully the marshals would end this ordeal with Todd Burk once and for all.

Ashley hurried up the porch steps, past a brooding Rip, and opened the door. She stepped inside, but he stayed on the porch.

"What's wrong?" she asked. "I promise it's a good surprise. It won't upset you and we won't argue."

"It's just that you've lived in this house for five and a half years, I've been here countless times, but this is the first time I've come in through the front door."

She reached for him, taking him by the arm, and pulled him across the threshold. "Why did you always come around back?" She closed the door, locked it and put on the chain.

"You didn't seem thrilled about my visits. In case your family or a friend stopped by, I figured it would be best if they didn't see my bike."

She took his hand. "I felt like you were just as bad as my parents, checking up on me, giving me a hard time for living out here by myself."

"A young, pretty woman living alone with no neighbor in shouting distance tended to worry me. A lot."

She led him down the hall. "It made me feel like you underestimated me. My ability to handle myself if something were to happen."

"I never underestimated you, Ash. I just prefer to over-estimate other people's capacity for evil."

"Guess I didn't think of it that way." She stopped in front of her bedroom. Holding his gaze, she backed up into the room, tugging him along with her.

He halted in the doorway. "What are you doing?"

"At first, I was annoyed when you'd stop by, but after a while, I looked forward to your visits. Every time I heard the rumble of your bike coming, pulling around back, I'd get these electric tingles and a part of me couldn't wait to see you."

"You hid it well."

"I'm sorry. I just wanted to be sure this thing between us was real, and not you trying to manipulate me, or use me because I was a cop. That you really wanted to see Burk in jail. It was taking you so long to handle him."

"Revenge would've been easy, but you wanted justice. He was slipperier than I anticipated."

She set her purse on the dresser and held out her hand for him.

Rip sighed like the weight of the world rested on his shoulders. "Why are you doing this? I have to leave. Soon. Your family, your job, your life, are here."

"You're asking the wrong question. Ask me the right one. The one from the motel."

His gaze bore into hers. "What am I to you?"

She took a deep breath, but she wasn't confused or un-sure. This time she was certain of her answer. "You're my anchor. The one I confide in." She shared so many things with him first, some she'd never even told her parents. Wanting to be a deputy. Enrolling in college. The problem she had with a sexist professor. Her worst nightmare—that the authorities would never get Burk. How she wanted to get married and have a couple of kids. That she avoided monthly karaoke night with the sheriff's office and Laramie Fire Department because she had an irrational fear of singing in public and only did it at home. "The one person who has *been* there for me. Protecting me. Helping me. Sacrificing for me." She didn't realize she was moving toward him until she was touching him. "This thing between us hasn't been conventional, but it's real and I'd be lost without it. Without you." She took another deep breath. "Because I love you."

Nothing had ever felt so right or sounded so true. She eased further back into her bedroom.

And this time, he followed. "You shouldn't say those words lightly."

"I haven't."

He took her in his arms. "I want more than a night."

"I know." She slipped his jacket off, letting it hit the floor, and then hers.

"I want everything with you."

She unbuckled his belt, transfixed by his piercing gaze. "Then we're on the same page."

"But how? What about your job? Your family?"

Putting her hands on his cheeks, the scratchy stubble forming a beard tickling her palms, she brought his face to hers. "We're going to be together. We'll discuss the details later." After they made love.

His mouth took hers and he kissed her, a deep, sensual kiss that had her moaning and losing her balance. Digging her hands into the material of his shirt, she wanted him inside her, no long foreplay, only the fast, frantic rush of passion. She pulled the Henley over his head and started unbuttoning her shirt.

"Wait," he said, and she hoped he wasn't going to come

up with another reason why they couldn't be together. "We're going to do this slow and easy. I want you to remember the first time I make love to you. For it to burn in your memory for all the days and nights to come."

The first time I make love to you. There would be other times, other ways they'd do this.

"You hide it well."

"What?"

"Being such a romantic."

He caressed her cheek and gave her a soft grin. "Do you still have any of those bath oils and candles I bought you?"

She nodded. He bought her the most luxurious gifts. She only used them on special occasions, savoring them. "The oils are in the bathroom. I'll light the candles."

Not only was he a generous lover but a romantic, too. Jasper hadn't taken it slowly or thought of her pleasure. Within minutes, it had been done, and she hadn't felt any different, even though she was no longer a virgin.

But this…making love to Rip would change everything.

He went into the bathroom and started the water. She dug out the large, scented soy candles that smelled like a lush tropical paradise and lit them. She set one on each nightstand and carried the other two to the bathroom, where she found Rip standing in all his glory, without a stitch of clothing on.

Her mouth dropped. He was beautiful. Rugged. A work of art she couldn't wait to get her hands on. "No fair, I wanted to undress you."

"Next time." He took the candles from her and set them down. They reflected a soft white light in the mirror, providing the only illumination in the room. "There is one thing," he said.

No, no, no. "This is happening, Rip."

He smiled and it was a rainbow after a storm, glorious

and filled with promise. The hot look in his eyes sparked heat low in her abdomen. "I don't have protection. I didn't plan on this."

Oh, not what she was expecting him to say. "I used a condom with Jasper."

"Please refrain from mentioning other men when I'm naked and about to make love to you."

"Sorry," she said with a shake of her head. "Anyway, I had a checkup after." She pressed her hand to the heavy stubble lining his jaw, enjoying the way it scratched her palm. "I'm clean and I take the pill."

His eyes changed. The desire from before turned even darker. "It's been a while for me, but I'm clean, too."

"Then I don't want there to be anything between us."

No barriers. No past. No secrets. Just the two of them. She wanted to open her soul to him.

He stripped off her shirt and unfastened her bra. Crouching, he pressed kisses to her stomach before slipping off her shoes. He unbuttoned her jeans and pulled them down. She touched the top of his head, balancing herself as he tugged them off.

Her knees trembled. Who was she kidding? She trembled all over.

Rip planted a kiss at the apex between her thighs, his warm breath coursing through the silky material of her panties, unraveling her in thirteen different ways. Then he gripped the waistband and slid them down, allowing her to step out of them. Leaving them on the floor, he stood and looked at her.

Fixing her attention on his mouth, the shape of his full lips, the sexy crook of his smile, she shivered. Grabbing a clip from the counter, she pinned her hair on top of her head while he shut off the faucet and checked the temperature.

Rip held out a hand, helping her into the claw-footed porcelain tub filled with bubbles that smelled divine. He climbed in on the other side, the water sloshing, and eased down, careful not to get his bandaged hand wet. His legs stretched out, and she clamped her knees together, making room for him to surround her.

In the candlelight suffusing the room, he bathed her gently, tenderly, caressing every inch of skin. No one had ever taken such care of her. Been so patient with his affection. And when he finished, she bathed him. She was familiar with the top half of his body but enjoyed the new spots she hadn't yet explored. Stroking him in places that made him groan, and she understood what he meant about liking to hear her pleasure because hearing his lit her up inside.

Every kiss, every touch, every stroke heated them until their desire for each other reached a torturous simmer. She was ready to climb on top of him and have him right there in the tub. His restraint was phenomenal.

"I can't wait any longer," she admitted.

Another heartrending smile. "Me neither."

They got out and hurried, towel-drying each other off.

Rip bent over and scooped her up off the floor, lifting her in his arms.

"You'll hurt your hand," she said, worried about him. "And what about your head?"

He was already moving out of the bathroom and set her down on the bed. "I've got this."

She scooted higher on the bed and lay back. He climbed up, prowling closer.

Excitement pulsed through her and goose bumps pebbled her skin.

Island scents drifted in the air—Tahitian vanilla, white musk, night-blooming jasmine. He settled between her spread legs, caressed her cheek with the knuckle of his index finger, moved to her mouth and stroked her bottom lip with his thumb. She caught the tip between her teeth, bit down lightly, and sucked.

"God, you are amazing," he said, his voice filled with the same awe she felt looking at him. "So sexy."

He kissed her, a searing brand of possession and passion, his hand diving between them, his fingers stroking that place she ached most. He knew precisely how to caress her to make the rush of desire flood her body, to make her tremble with longing, and she became lost. So sweetly lost in him. And this time the pleasure was both theirs to share.

His thigh settled between her legs, and she opened herself, pressing the warmth of her most intimate spot against him. Desire roared through her, so intense, so urgent, she swore the world quaked.

Need took over as he entered her slowly. She cried out, not in pain but in a kind of triumph. Gripping his hips, she urged him to move faster, deeper. Sensation swamped her with a force she'd never felt before and she wanted more. Lots more.

They rocked together as one, clinging to each other, breathing hard, climbing higher. Not just having sex or hooking up or having a fling but making love. Committing to each other.

This new dimension of their relationship was sensual and nurturing and hot and better than she'd imagined. All these years she'd been searching for something she couldn't fully define, and here she'd found it in the one man who had been there for her all along.

Rip.

Chapter Eighteen

Holding Ash in his arms, in her bed, Rip felt like he'd won the lottery. If this was a dream, he never wanted to wake from it. "How do you feel?"

"Different. Revered and ravaged," she said, and he laughed. "I wish I had waited for you. Waited for this. Instead of blowing my first time on Jasper."

He patted her butt softly, playfully. "Please, do me the favor of not mentioning him again. Ever."

"Okay, okay. But I will say one more thing."

Rip groaned.

"You'll appreciate this. You gave me my first orgasm, in the motel," she said, and he did appreciate it.

"Well, I've given you plenty of those. Five so far, not that I'm counting, and more to come. Pun intended."

She elbowed him lightly in his side. "Humble. But I am looking forward to lots of other firsts with you, like our bath." She rolled on top of him and peered down into his face. "Have you ever been married?"

"Yes." Suddenly, he wished he had been the one who'd waited for her. "It was right after I became a Raider. Spec Ops. The marriage lasted less than two years. She couldn't handle me being gone all the time. Didn't like being lonely. I came back from a deployment to find her living with another guy." The memory no longer stung. It had happened a lifetime ago.

"What was she like? I mean, what's your type?"

"You're my type." He slid his arms around her waist. "Beautiful, bold, brave. Loyal." Mandy had only been pretty. He'd been in lust with her, mistaking it for love. His ego had been more hurt than his heart when the marriage ended.

"So, I won't be your first wife," she said, and the sadness in her tone and her eyes stopped him from making a joke about how he'd never promised marriage.

"No. Not the first. But the last. The only one to matter. My dad used to talk about how my mom was the great love of his life. You're mine." He kissed her. "I love you. I have for a few years."

"Did you fall in love with me before or after you started bringing me tacos?"

"I *wanted* you before the tacos, but I think I realized I'd fallen in deep when I started bringing you candles and bath oils and—"

"And the booze."

He chuckled. "Yeah."

"There was one night," she said, slipping her leg between his and snuggling against him, "where I wanted you so bad, I came close to inviting you to my bedroom."

"Why didn't you?"

"You called me deputy and it…shifted my thoughts back into alignment."

"That's why I did it. Called you deputy all the time. To keep me focused on not crossing the line between us." He put a knuckle under her chin and tipped her face up, so he could look into her eyes. "Speaking of which, what about your job?"

Sighing, she rolled off him onto her back and stared

up at the ceiling. At the lack of eye contact, he braced for what she might say.

"Don't get upset, but the sheriff suspended me because I misled him about the DEA mission, and the current status of our relationship prompted an investigation."

"What?" He leaned up on his forearm and peered down at her face. "I can talk to him. Try to clear it up."

She pressed her index finger to his lips. "I'm not worried about the internal investigation. I'll be cleared, but I still quit."

He moved her finger from his mouth. "Ash, you can't."

"I already did. The sheriff asked me to reconsider, said he didn't want to lose a good deputy and that the investigation was only procedural. I told him that a law enforcement officer has to do things by the book. But to get Todd, it required me to bend the rules. I had to work in the gray. I don't regret it and I also don't think I should wear the badge anymore. Todd was arrested and when he's found, he won't slip out of those charges. He was the only reason I became a deputy in the first place. I achieved what I set out to do. You were in the hospital, and suddenly, you were all that mattered to me. So, I quit. It's done. Tomorrow, we'll tell my parents and Ida that we have to leave. Together. Besides, I can find a new job wherever we decide to make our new home. Not law enforcement of course, but something to help people that also pays the bills."

He wrapped an arm around her waist. "You don't have to worry about paying bills. I bring in plenty of money."

Turning onto her side, facing him, she raised an eyebrow. "Clean, legit money?"

He chuckled. "Yeah, of course. I started a company. Ironside Protection Services."

"I've heard of it. That's you? How were you able to hide

being the owner from the DEA? It didn't come up in their deep dive on you."

"I was Special Forces. I know how to hide things I don't want others to know. Over the years, I've expanded a great deal into Montana, Idaho and Colorado. I employee a lot of veterans."

"Guess I could do protection work."

He trailed his fingers over her spine, loving the feel of her nestled against him. "I bring in close to a million a year. You can do what you want. Handle management. Source intel. Lead a team. Stay home with me and we can practice making babies."

She sat up and stared down at him. "A million *dollars* a year?"

"Yep."

"And you pay your taxes?"

He laughed. "On time. Every year. I swear it's all aboveboard. You can trust me, honey."

"I know I can. It's just I had no idea."

"That's the point. For no one to know."

"You're full of surprises. The good kind." She gave him a peck on the lips and hopped out of the bed. "I'm going to go to the bathroom and clean up."

"I'm starving."

"There's a strawberry rhubarb pie on the counter and shepherd's pie in the fridge."

"Both are my favorite."

"I'm aware. I've been paying attention, too, over the years and I had planned for you to stay here. The strawberry rhubarb is from the Divine Treats café and the shepherd's pie is from my mother's kitchen."

He pulled on his boxer briefs. "Want anything?"

"Glass of water." She paused, thinking. "Ooh, this is

a night to celebrate. Calls for Clase Azul. I'll meet you in the kitchen. Give me a couple of minutes." She disappeared in the bathroom, shutting the door, and he heard the faucet turn on.

His head buzzed. Not from pain. Not from swelling. From this high of being in love, of knowing that Ash loved him back, wanted to build a life together.

He padded down the hall, passing her living room, and entered the kitchen.

A draft sent a chill over him. The back door creaked. Slightly ajar. The bottom windowpane had been busted in, broken glass on the floor.

Then he sensed movement behind him before he heard it.

He grabbed the first thing within reach—a cast-iron skillet from the dish rack on the counter—and swung around.

The iron pan collided with the barrel of a twelve-gauge shotgun that Freddy was holding. A blast exploded, shattering the window over the sink.

Rip swung again, smashing the pan against Freddy's fingers and then across his head, sending him to the floor in a whirling sprawl.

Heavyset Clive had a baseball bat. Tall, burly Arlo limped forward, raising a 9mm.

Over their shoulders, Rip glimpsed Todd Burk stalking down the hallway toward the bedroom.

"Ashley!" Rip ducked, taking cover behind the kitchen island as Arlo opened fire. He grabbed the shotgun from an unconscious Freddy.

When those men, former brothers, had attacked him at his home, he'd gone easy, only dislocating a kneecap.

Now they were here, going after Ash, and he'd show no mercy.

Singing to herself in the mirror, she wondered where they'd go, if he already had a city or town picked out. Would they even stay in Wyoming?

Boom.

"What the hell?" She shut off the water and listened.

"Ashley!"

Her heart stuttered. *Rip.*

She snatched the long purple kimono robe from the hook on the back of the door, put it on and tied the belt.

Gunfire erupted deeper in the house, from the kitchen, sending her pulse skyrocketing. She opened the bathroom door and froze. Todd Burk stood on the other side. In her bedroom. His black hair was wild, his eyes crazed. He had her in height, he had her in weight, and he was holding a hammer.

In milliseconds, she located her gun and pepper spray. Both in her purse. On top of the dresser that Todd had pushed in front of the closed bedroom door.

Panic wanted to ice her brain. It snaked through her belly, slithered up her throat, made her hands shake until she balled them into fists. Fear threatened to swallow her, but her anger, her seven years of grief, her bottled-up pain were stronger.

A vicious smirk tugged at his mouth, and he raised the hammer.

She kicked him in the crotch as hard as she could. As he doubled over, she rammed the fleshy part of her palm up into his nose. Once. Twice. Bone crunched. Then she kicked him again, this time thrusting the heel of her foot into his gut, shoving him back, putting space between them.

More gunfire came from the kitchen.

Todd stumbled and fell near the dresser, blocking her

escape, but the hammer slipped from his grip and clattered to the hardwood floor.

She bolted for her nightstand on the other side of the room.

Cursing and grunting, Todd was up. He leaped onto the bed with the hammer in his hand.

She grabbed the handle of her top drawer and pulled it open, but Todd lunged, taking her down to the floor. The breath was knocked from her. Lights starred behind her eyes when her head rapped hard against the floor. She still held the handle, but the drawer had been yanked free from the nightstand, the contents spilling around her.

She felt around for what she was looking for. She'd seen it fall to her left.

Crouched on top of her, Todd raised the hammer. She swung her forearm into his head, across his face. A move Rip had taught her after she graduated from the academy to keep her from breaking her hand. Then she went for his eyes, raked furrows down his cheek.

He howled like a wounded animal. Ashley grabbed his arm holding the hammer with her hands and bit him, as hard as she could, drawing blood.

The hammer fell, but with his free hand, he punched her. The blow stunned her, but she kept moving.

His bloody hand was shaking. She only wished she'd been able to take off a finger.

Head clearing, she scrambled with him for the hammer. His hand closed over it first, but she didn't stop fighting for it.

"The boys are taking care of Rip. So you and I can play."

Todd's face was close to hers, his body pinning her in an obscene way. His wrist was slippery with his own blood.

She cursed as she lost her grip.

Smiling, in control of the hammer, he ripped open the top of her robe, exposing her breasts. "I want a taste of what Rip's been protecting all this time before I kill you."

She sagged, but reached out, searching the floor with her fingers, hoping, praying, the weapon might be nearby.

There! She found it. Her hand closed around cool aluminum. "You're not man enough to take what's his."

A lecherous smile curled his lips and something in his eyes made her stomach clench like a fist. "We'll see when I'm done with you."

With her finger, she flipped the on switch. Blue sparks snapped and sizzled, drawing his gaze down to her hand.

She shoved the stun gun into his side.

Todd let out a piercing wail, falling off her to the side, shuddering and convulsing. The hammer dropped to the floor.

One to two seconds of contact caused unbearable pain, muscle cramps and dizziness. She shocked him again. Todd and his flunkies had broken into her house, assuming she was alone and weak. They had been thinking four against one. Had planned to do unspeakable things to her and then kill her.

A geyser of pain and rage welled up in her and exploded. She hit him with her fists. In the face. In the gut. In the stomach. Screaming, she kept punching. The red haze clouding her vision darkened every time she landed a blow.

She never heard Rip calling her name. Or the battering of the door. Or him busting it down and shoving the dresser aside.

His arms were around her waist, her back pressed to his chest, and he was hauling her off Todd. She was still swinging and kicking when he carried her to the corner of the room.

"Ashley!"

She wasn't sure how many times he'd yelled her name before it registered.

"Look at me. Not him."

Chest heaving, she tore her gaze from the sight of Todd, crumpled and bleeding on her floor, to Rip. Met his eyes. Those riveting blue-gray eyes anchored her. The immediate connection calmed her. The red haze of fury dissipated, and tears fell from her eyes.

"I need to know. Right now," Rip said.

"What? Know what?" Then she realized he'd been talking to her, but she hadn't heard him.

"Todd Burk. Do you want him dead…or in prison? I need to know, right now before I call 911."

She glanced back at the man who had killed her brother, who had caused her family unfathomable suffering.

"Look at me when you decide." Rip's voice was sharp, sobering.

Finding his gaze and holding it, she took a long, ragged breath. "I want him to burn in hell for what he's done." Staying focused on this man, whom she loved, whom she was safe with, who would do anything for her, she then thought about her brother, remembered the promises she'd made her parents when she joined the sheriff's office. "But I want him to rot in jail first."

She wanted justice.

Not vengeance.

"Good choice, honey." He sat her down in a chair. Yanked a cord from the lamp on the bedside table. Tied Todd's hands behind his back. Ran from the room for a minute. Hurried back with duct tape and a phone pressed to his ear. "The four escapees the marshals are searching for broke in and attacked us. I believe the officer outside is dead."

Rip finished the call on speakerphone, giving the 911 operator Ashley's address, as he doubled the restraints on Todd's wrists with the tape and bound his ankles.

He grabbed their clothes and ushered her to the hall. Quickly, he dressed her and himself. Looking her over, he wiped blood from her face, and she winced from the tenderness in her cheek where Todd had hit her.

"Sorry I didn't get to you sooner," he said, regret heavy in his voice.

She leaned against him, needing his strength, his support, and he wrapped her in a bear hug. "He had a hammer. He was going to rape me." She shivered at the prospect of what might have happened if Rip hadn't been in the house. But he had been there dealing with the others. "I don't know what choice I would have made if you hadn't stopped me."

"I do. You would've made the right one." He tightened the embrace. "I believe that. I believe in you."

"But how can you? After the way I hit him. I didn't think I'd be able to stop."

"Todd had that coming and deserved everything you dished out. Deserves far worse. But I know because in all the years when you weren't sure what side of the law I was on, you never asked me to put him down like a dog, shoot him unaware in the back and bury him in a deep hole somewhere no one would find him. You never would have."

It had crossed her mind, but she could never bring herself to utter the words. To ask someone to commit murder. Not that Rip would have ever gone through with it. He was a good man, the best kind of man, who believed in justice. Not revenge. "What about the others?"

"Two are still breathing, but they're broken. They're going to have a tough time in prison wearing casts."

She pressed her head to his chest. "I'm glad it's over. I'm glad you're here."

"I'm the one who's glad. That you're safe and okay."

"What if you hadn't stayed? What if you had gone back to your trailer?" A shudder racked her body.

"But I'm here. Because you're stubborn and persistent. Because you had the guts to tell me how you felt about me and then had your way with me in bed to get me to stay."

Pulling back and looking up at him, she gave him a grim smile.

"That's my Ash, head held high, a warrior to the bone." He took her chin between his thumb and index finger. "I'm never leaving you again. It's you and me together from now on."

She nodded. "Together."

He lowered his mouth to hers and kissed her, long and slow and deep, and her heart melted as everything else faded away.

Ten months later

RIP STOOD BESIDE ASH, with his arm around her shoulder, in front of Ida Hindley's grave in Millstone Cemetery. Though he couldn't be with Ida during her last months, he was comforted knowing that she had lived to see her ninetieth birthday, and in the end, had been surrounded by love and hadn't been alone, thanks to Ashley's parents.

"It was a lovely service," Ashley's mother said to the small group.

Only her parents, Quill and JD had been invited. An announcement about her passing would be put in the paper along with her obituary once Rip and Ash left town again. They'd only flown in for the funeral.

"Of course, it was." Rip smiled, looking at her simple headstone that read *Ida Hindley, Beloved Wife, Mother, Auntie and Friend*, along with the years of her birth and death. "Auntie Ida planned it herself. She claimed it was so I wouldn't have to do it and that's partly true, but she was also a perfectionist and wanted it done right."

Ashley's father laughed. "Even when it came to making the bed. If I didn't do hospital corners, it was done wrong."

Fond memories sprang to mind and his chest filled with gratitude and love. "Thanks to her, making a bed and shooting were the two things I didn't have to worry about learning how to do when I joined the Marines."

"She was a good woman," Quill said.

"With Rip and Ashley gone, Ida appreciated you two paying her visits," Mrs. Russo said to Quill and JD.

JD nodded. "She played a mean hand of pinochle and enjoyed taking our money."

"I didn't know pinochle was a gambling game," Ash said, resting her head on Rip.

Quill laughed. "It was the way Ida played it."

"Tired?" Rip asked Ash, tightening his arm around her.

"Starving." She put her hands on her belly, nearly the size of a basketball, and rubbed. Her wedding ring, a diamond eternity band, sparkled, catching the light. "I'm always hungry."

"I was the same when I was pregnant." Her mother put a hand on Ash's rounded tummy. "You said you'd tell us the sex in person. We've been waiting."

"What are you having, man?" Quill stepped closer. "Boy or girl?"

Rip looked at her. "Do you want to tell them or should I?"

Ash shrugged, a mischievous gleam in her eye. "Let's do it at the same time. One, two, three. Boy."

"Girl."

Everyone looked at them, confused.

Her father's face lit up. "Oh, my! Twins? Is my jelly bean having two beans?"

Ash nodded. "A boy and a girl."

Everyone took turns giving them hugs and offering congratulations.

Then her mom broke down in tears.

"Don't cry." Ash kissed her cheek and comforted her. "This is good news."

"The best news possible." Her mom sniffled. "It's just that your dad and I retired early. With Ida gone, we have no reason to stay here. We miss you. We want to see the baby, the babies when they're born, watch them grow up, but…"

Rip took out a handkerchief and gave it to her. "Ash and I have been talking about that. We were wondering if you wanted to come live with us. Well, not in the same house. But walking distance close."

Her mother went slack-jawed with surprise and looked at Ash as if to check whether the proposal was real.

"Yes, Mom. We want you guys with us if that's what you want."

Ash had broached the subject and he had been open to it. They had even made plans to bring Ida. He'd always wanted a big family. If he could give his kids grandparents, who wanted to be hands-on and in their lives every day, then he would. It was also a huge plus that he'd make his wife ecstatic in the process.

An easy win-win.

Her father grabbed him in a bear hug. "Thank you, Rip."

"Sir, you're more than welcome. We're happy to have you."

"We told you at the wedding. No more sir or ma'am or

Mr. and Mrs. Russo. It's Dante and Emily. Or if you'd prefer, Mom and Dad. You're not our son-in-law, but our son."

They'd gotten legally married at the Justice of the Peace in the United States, only the two of them. Then had a small ceremony in Paris with Ash's parents and Auntie Ida. At the Place du Trocadéro, overlooking the Eiffel Tower. Ash had wanted to do it in Europe, since she'd never been, and he thought she'd love it. Her parents and Ida had been impressed and her mother couldn't stop crying happy tears. For their honeymoon, they'd traveled for a month, going wherever Ash wanted.

"All right. No more formalities." Rip nodded, sticky emotions surfacing. He'd have to work his way up to calling them Mom and Dad. "Don't sell your house. Don't change your routine. Just have two bags packed and ready. One day, we'll call with instructions. Follow them to the letter. Don't say goodbye to anyone. Okay?" It was similar to how he'd handled things for the wedding. The obstetrician thought the babies might come early. He was planning for a December birth and to have her parents relocated by Thanksgiving.

"Yes, yes," Dante and Emily both said.

"Will we ever see you guys again?" JD asked.

The district attorney had plenty of evidence to put Todd, Freddy and Arlo away, including for the murder of the police officer who had been assigned to protect them. Clive hadn't left Ash's house alive. Fortunately, the case was so solid against the others it didn't require either of their testimonies in court. Their sworn affidavits would suffice. Many of the Sons of Chaos had been arrested, including Stryker, when the prostitution ring was busted. But the Sandoval cartel was still a potential problem waiting to happen.

"No, you won't." Rip shook his head. "I'm sorry."

"We understand." Quill patted him on the back. "Thanks for still kicking Ironside work to the Warriors."

"It'll help keep the club legit," JD said, proudly wearing his president patch.

"Now that's all settled, can we eat?" Ash asked.

"Let's go to the house," Emily said. "I have plenty of food prepared."

"Good. I'm hungry." Quill patted his own round belly, heading for his bike.

Once they finished lunch, they would go to the Laramie Regional Airport, where Rip had a chartered plane waiting. Staying any longer than the day wasn't wise. Not a chance he was willing to take with his family, now that the cartel knew his name and involvement in the seizure of the drug camp.

They started for the car when Ash stopped suddenly.

"The babies are kicking." She put his hand on her belly.

After a second or two he felt it. Like a powerful one-two jab from inside her. Took his breath away every time. "They're so strong."

She smiled. "Fighters like their dad."

"And their mom."

"I was thinking about names. How about Hatch Angelo and Elizabeth Ida?"

The suggestions warmed his heart, choking him up in a way he didn't expect. This beautiful woman never stopped surprising him in the best ways. He nodded. "Great choices, but only if you really love those names."

She pressed a palm to his clean-shaven cheek. "I love you. And I think those names would make us both happy."

"Thank you. For loving me. For marrying me. For giving me this family I've always wanted." Far too long he'd been looking to the motorcycle club and the Marine Corps to give him that intangible piece missing to make him feel whole. But this was it. Ashley, the babies, her parents, even Quill and JD. This was what he'd been missing.

"I wish I'd seen it sooner," she said. "How remarkable you are. Seen that I could trust you. That we were meant to be."

No, he rejected that. Immediately. He looped his arms around her and pulled her close. "Everything happened as it was supposed to. Without all that came before, we would never have been here. Sometimes things have to happen, to push us, to show us, to get us where we never thought we'd be."

Not in a million years had he thought it possible for Ash to be his wife and the mother of his children, that he would even ever be a father.

"Then I'd go through it again." She stared at him with light and love. "All seven years. Walking through fire. To get to the other side, to be here with you now."

He really had won the lottery, because Ash was the remarkable one.

The great love of his life.

* * * * *